Cold Iron

Ghost Stories from the 21st Century

Editors
Eileen Jones
Peter Mortimer

First published 2017 by IRON Press
5 Marden Terrace
Cullercoats
North Shields
NE30 4PD
tel/fax +44(0)191 2531901
ironpress@blueyonder.co.uk
www.ironpress.co.uk

ISBN 9780993124587
Printed by imprintdigital.com

Stories © Individual Author 2017
This collection © IRON Press 2017

Cover Illustration Ryan Foston
Cover and Book Design Brian Grogan

Typeset in Georgia
IRON Press books are distributed by NBNI International
and represented by Inpress Ltd
Churchill House, 12 Mosley Street,
Newcastle upon Tyne, NE1 1DE
tel: +44(0)191 2308104
www.inpressbooks.co.uk

Introduction

Jointly editing this collection has been a pleasurable, if exacting, task. We both read all of the submitted stories (almost 200) and each one was discussed during a four month period in which we drew up a short list, then an even shorter list, settling finally on the seventeen you have awaiting you in this collection. During this time, many packets of Ringtons tea were consumed. Several well-known names didn't make it, while some total unknowns did, which seems fair enough. The longer the selection process continued, the more the final selection began to shape itself. Some stories that were written elegantly enough and were perfectly presentable were declined because they didn't quite belong in an anthology of this title. Many writers seemed locked into their idea of what a ghost story 'should' be, whereas our only general stipulation was that the story should contain a ghost. The word 'ghost' is open to many interpretations, of course. Instead of trying strictly to define it, we treated each equivocal case in its own right, often trusting to our instincts.

Some modern ghost story writers successfully include in their collections stories which have entirely historical characters and settings, and links with contemporary life firmly in the subtext. But what excited us was the prospect of adapting this most traditional of genres to our present era, in the most direct way. Of course, this in itself is something of a tradition. Charles Dickens' second most famous ghost story, *The Signalman*, published in 1866, was very much of its time — and likely inspired by real events, including his own traumatic experience of the derailment at Staplehurst, Kent in 1865. Perhaps more significantly, Dickens was exploiting the ghostly potential of the isolation of the signal box and the railway tunnel darkness, and the spookiness of telegraphic communication at a time when the horrific signal related Clayburn crash of 1861 would be still vivid in his readers' minds. The supernatural events in M.R. James' tales, clearly had their origins in his medieval studies, but his protagonists were usually firmly rooted in his everyday world of the early 20th century—here he was using the contrast between the two worlds to scary effect. A near contemporary of James, E.F. Benson (of Mapp & Lucia fame) makes the same device explicit in his best known 'spook' tale, *The Bus Conductor*, where the narrator asks his haunted friend: 'You saw the ghost here, in this square box of a house on a modern street?'

The writers who interested us were those who took on both the responsibility of a ghost story and a sense of our own time and culture. Thus we liked very much the young couples in Jane Ayrie's and Michael Parker's stories, whose 21st century concerns are set against encounters with ghostly light effects (*The Light Left*) and the ancient wrath of a dispossessed widow (*Appropriation*). In *The Last Checkout* Wendy Robertson's ghost puts in a shift or two at a supermarket, Noreen Rees' ghost in *The Installation* is an ultra helpful tv engineer, and Tom Johnstone's revenant in *The Follow Up* has met her end via a mishap with a state of the art ride-on lawnmower.

Not all the stories are high drama. The ghost story is less likely than its close relation, the horror story, to depend on climactic shock or fear. Sometimes atmosphere itself is disturbing. In *How to be Invisible,* Chris Barnham's protagonist begins to inhabit a ghostly dimension following a break up. As his life falls apart, he starts, perhaps literally, to fade from view. It's not surprising that in the 21st century the newest meaning of 'ghost' has emerged online, where 'to ghost' is to subject a former 'friend' to the living 'death' of exclusion from social media. Matt Wesolowski uses this concept to excellent effect in *Ghosted*.

No doubt the ghost story genre will continue to survive the increasing pace of modernity. In our various ways, we're all haunted and we can all suffer from feelings of alienation. The best ghost stories can evoke those hauntings and those feelings anywhere: in a graveyard encounter between contemporary young offenders and ghostly First World War veterans (Christine D. Goodwin's *Dulce et Decorum)*; in a modern cancer ward (Kitty Fitzgerald's *Intruder*)*;* in a football stand in Ian Harris' *Support You Evermore*; or sitting screen bound in today's version of the 'square box of a house on a modern street'.

Eileen Jones, Peter Mortimer
Editors
Tyneside, Summer 2017

The Stories

Page		
7	The Last Checkout	Wendy Robertson
16	Support You Ever More	Ian Harris
23	Intruder	Kitty Fitzgerald
30	How to be Invisible	Chris Barnham
38	The Undertaker's Boy	Karen Turner
45	Playing in Their Own Time	Tracy Fahey
56	Sunday Lunch	Jenny Cozens
63	Dulce et Decorum	Christine D. Goodwin
71	The Installation	Noreen Rees
78	A Trick of the Light	Andrew Jones
83	Appropriation	Michael James Parker
91	The Lengthsman	Charles Wilkinson
99	The Light Left	Jane Ayrie
108	Ghosted	Matt Wesolowski
117	In the Blink of an Eye	Beda Higgins
124	The Follow Up	Tom Johnstone
131	The Last Bus Home	Andrea Stephenson

Dedicated to all true spirits

The Last Checkout
Wendy Robertson

WENDY ROBERTSON first embraced teaching as a creative and quite successful enterprise but was always a 'writer who happened to teach' – publishing three novels while she was still teaching, as well as some short stories and journalism. After that she surrendered to the writing goddess and has published a wide range of novels and two short story collections as well as the occasional article. More on website: <www.lifewicetasted.blogspot.co.uk>.

ESME'S HUSBAND MAURICE died when they were both thirty-five. No, Esme would say. It was on her birthday, so it must have been six days earlier. After all wasn't she six days older than Maurice? Always had been, ever since she'd got on with him at that sixth form dance. Tall, blond and graceful, Maurice was the pick of the crop even though he didn't dance.

By the time they'd been married for three years Esme had learned that Maurice – the meticulous son of a meticulous mother – liked routine: Monday, fry up of Sunday's dinner leftovers; Wednesday mince and dumplings; Friday night fish and chips; Saturday night the pub then early to bed for the energetic wrestling match Maurice called making love. When Esme – in the early days of their marriage – suggested a midweek tumble, he shook his head. 'Not on a work night, Es,' he would say. 'Not on a work night.' That was down to something he'd read about boxers. Or was it footballers?

Maurice didn't like any kind of change. A new road in the town and he was growling, spitting feathers. A change in a hospital appointment and he would propose manning the barricades. Foreigners in the town and he was in despair. Predictably, he canvassed for Nigel Farage and voted for Brexit.

Esme came to understand that Maurice and their life together was all of a piece. Children never turned up but neither of them mentioned it. His job – clerk to the council – was the big one. Her job – assistant librarian – was the small one.

Her old friends – who soon dropped away – wondered how a person like Esme – a little bit dizzy and loving the world: young people, old people, children, dogs, cats - could share her life with a man like that.

It turned out that Maurice's iron-clad routines came to be Esme's safety net. As long as she serviced Maurice's routines, he went his own sweet way and she went hers. She did her job in the little library three days a week where she was popular with the readers. On Tuesdays she went to her yoga at the college and on Thursdays she attended her knitting club at Costa Coffee. There she talked with the women and got to know a man who knitted in wild colours but said not a word.

One Thursday she was hurrying back from her knitting club to put a steak pie in the oven when she turned a corner onto the High Street and bumped into a young woman wearing a close headscarf who had a canvas bag filled with copies of the *Big Issue*.

'Sorry, so sorry!' Esme was flustered. The woman flashed her a twinkling smile. 'Is no matter,' she said. When her smile faded, her face had a closed, Madonna look. Esme bought a copy of the *Big Issue* and later, after supper, she stayed in the kitchen and read it from cover to cover. There on those pages lay life on the edge of everything and what could happen for people to put things right in society. And there were some nice photos too, of people just like the girl in her street, making an effort to make a living.

'Esme!' Maurice called from the sitting room. 'News!' They never missed the news. Maurice liked to keep up with things out there in the world. His current preoccupation was all those people getting into England through Calais. The French were at fault of course.

That week in the street she met the young woman again and they exchanged smiles and greetings. Esme asked how she was. 'Am a bit tired,' she said. 'I come a long way here on bus. Sometimes maybe not make enough for fare.'

Esme frowned. 'That's not right.'

The young woman shrugged. 'Is OK. I always make a little bit. I need for my little ones.'

'You have children?' said Esme astonished.

The girl spread three graceful brown fingers, held them in the air and smiled. 'One – two – three,' she said. 'Girls. Next time boy!' She rolled up a *Big Issue* and handed it to Esme, who gave her a five pound note and rejected the change.

Esme walked on to the café on the corner and read the paper. After that day she would buy the *Big Issue* every week and read it in the café. She usually put the paper in the bin as soon as she got home. One week Maurice, who loved the recycling ritual, came across a discarded *Big Issue*. He came into the kitchen where Esme was clearing away the detritus from their Wednesday mince-and dumplings. 'What's this? What's this?' He shouted, his face a dangerous shade of purple.

She looked carefully at the paper clutched in his hand. 'It's the *Big Issue*,' she said. 'I buy it every week.'

'You bought it off some foreign street beggar? And then hid it away?'

Esme stood very straight. 'I didn't hide it, Maurice. I knew you wouldn't want to read it so I...'

He flung it onto the table and shook his head, making his thick fair hair lift in the air. 'I swear I don't know where you go to, Es, in that head of yours.' He turned and stalked off into the hallway. And then Esme heard a crack. She rushed after him and nearly fell over him where he lay collapsed on the floor, his face stiff and white and one hand fluttering.

Maurice's mother Greta came to stay and took charge of the funeral. She brought with her a framed photo of Maurice looking young and handsome. She made the *vol-au-vents* and sandwiches and supplied the port and sherry for the toasts at the wake. Maurice's boss, the mayor, paid tribute as did Peter, his friend, who had started working at the council with him.

Esme looked blankly around at the people in her long room. She watched Greta doing her rounds among them, graciously sharing everyone's sorrow and accepting everyone's sympathy. Esme wondered how Greta, managed not to let her sadness show. Esme looked at Maurice's photograph on the sideboard: the handsome young man she had married. So young.

Maurice's friend Peter caught her glance, broke off from his group and headed in Esme's direction. She backed away, leapt the stairs two at a time, went into her bedroom, and locked the door.

She sat on the bed and tried to feel something other than paralysis: an inability to think or feel. Anything. She sat until she could hear talk in the hallway and cars starting up outside. Finally, the front door slammed and everything went quiet. Then she could hear the tip tapping of Greta's high heels on the parquet on the landing. A gentle knock on the door. 'Esme? Everyone has left. They all understand that you must be grief stricken. Don't worry. They don't think it bad manners that you hid yourself away.'

Obviously Greta did. She coughed. 'Oh well. I'll leave you in peace. Stephen's coming at six to help me with Maurice's papers.' Stephen was Maurice's handsome younger brother. He'd been at the funeral but was so popular at the wake that he hadn't got round to talking to Esme.

Greta's footsteps tapped down the stairs and the front door slammed. Esme breathed out and stood up. She turned to the bed, placed the pillows neatly, dead centre. A bed for one. She dropped onto it, put her head on the pillows and went to sleep.

On Sunday Esme went to church and sat right at the back. At the end of the service the vicar – a stout, rough-spoken woman who had conducted Maurice's funeral – stopped beside Esme as she made her way to the back of the church. 'Are you bearing up, Mrs Cottrell?'

Esme shrugged.

'Always hard, I know. Have you cried yet?'

Esme shook her head.

The vicar nodded. 'That sometimes helps the ice to melt.' And she turned away to pay attention to someone tugging at her black gown.

When she got home though, Esme was very pleased she'd been to church.

At first she still followed Maurice's food routines even though she threw out a lot of food. She still paid a fiver for her *Big Issue* on Wednesdays, She still went to yoga at the college on Tuesdays and the Costa knitting club on Thursdays, before going on to do her shopping. The knitting women started to pull her into their talk. And the man there told her his name was Craig and showed her what he called his 'project' – images in wool of castles of the North, designed by himself. One Thursday, on her way to the shops, she closed her eyes feeling the wall of ice had started to melt around her.

In the supermarket that day she selected the chicken, the minced steak and the usual pork pie. Then it occurred to her that this was all such a waste and she turned the trolley round and returned all the food to their fridges. Then she moved on, picked three different cheeses, some salami, ham and tomatoes as well as her favourite green beans and avocados. Maurice had always sneered at avocados, calling them trendy: a favourite insult of his. Now Esme bought peaches and good coffee, realising that meals could just be a series of unplanned picnics.

She wheeled her trolley along the line of checkouts gagged up with queues. The last one, the one at the end, was empty. This was new. It was different to the others. More handsome, if you like, with dark wood panelling.

The young checkout girl wore the blue supermarket tunic with a matching close headscarf. She smiled up at Esme watching her unload her cheese and ham, her beans and avocados onto the counter. Esme frowned. For a moment she thought it was the *Big Issue* girl. But it wasn't. This girl was younger and she had a port wine mark on her neck shaped like a seahorse. Still she was very like the *Big Issue* girl.

Esme blurted. 'Are you new here? Have you worked here long?'

The girl smiled. A wisp of black hair escaped her headscarf. 'Only three days. Is a nice place to be. Here.' The voice was familiar.

'You have family here?'

'I have many here. Is like home.'

Esme loaded her shopping back onto the trolley. The bill came to forty-one pounds. She paid in cash: four ten pound notes and one fiver. The girl smiled up at her gave her the bill and four pound coins, and turned her attention to the next customer.

Esme wheeled the trolley outside and opened the boot of her little car. 'Excuse me madam?' A tall young man stood there, a security badge pinned onto his grey uniform shirt naming him *James Walton*.

'Yes?' she said, frowning.

'Mr Filey the manager says would you be kind enough to come and talk to him?'

'I don't think... I don't have the time.'

James Walton smiled genially. 'Mr Filey insists.' He took the handles of the trolley and started to wheel it towards the big doors.

Esme scurried along beside him. 'What is it?' she said. 'What's this about?'

'Don't worry madam. Mr Riley is a very kind man. Too kind, sometimes.'

She trudged silently alongside him to the store then, through the crowds, up in a lift to a cluttered office on the first floor. Mr Filey, short, and well turned out, stood up to greet her and pointed to the seat on the other side of his desk. James Walton wheeled her trolley beside Mr Filey and went to stand by the door, arms folded.

'Now Mrs...?

'Cottrell,' she supplied.

'Now, Mrs Cottrell I'm afraid it seems that you're guilty of theft.'

Esme's cheeks went red. 'That's not true. Absolutely not true.'

'You claim to have paid for the goods in this trolley?'

She reached for her purse. 'Of course I did. I paid in cash. I have the bill here.' She opened her purse. There was no bill. But lying crisply in her purse were the five ten pound notes she'd come out with. 'I... I paid. I swear...' Her voice trailed off.

James Walton came across, fiddled with Mr Riley's computer and turned the screen towards her. On the screen was the long line of checkouts. She watched herself wander to the end of the line. But there was no checkout with stylish wooden panels. Just a broad windowsill looking out over the car park. She watched herself smiling and talking as she loaded her shopping first onto the window sill and then back into the trolley.

Now she put her hands across her face. 'I didn't know. Where is that last checkout? That girl? There was a girl.'

Mr Riley shook his head. There is no last checkout Mrs Cottrell, and no girl.' He paused. 'I think you must have imagined it.' He stared at her bowed head for a long time, then coughed. 'I suggest, Mrs Cottrell you give James here the money and he'll pay for your goods and escort you to your car. Let's just say you had a bad moment. What these days they call an episode.'

As they went down in the lift, the security man grinned at her. 'Too kind. I told you he was too kind.'

'I didn't...' she blurted.

'Of course you didn't,' he purred, kindly enough.

He even helped Esme load her shopping into the boot of her car and waved her off as she bumped into gear. She parked outside the supermarket car park, put her head in her hands and took five very deep breaths. Then she went home and had a picnic tea of ham and cheese before she turned on the television to some documentary about the African Savannah.

Esme waited for the next Wednesday and made sure she was on the High Street early. The *Big Issue* girl was coming towards her, a small frown on her smooth brow.

'Hello!' said Esme. The girl pulled up short. Her smile was strained but still sweet. 'Good morning,' she said and put the heavy *Big Issue* bag on a raised wall surrounding a bit of garden. 'How are you today?'

'Good,' Esme said. 'To be honest I'm a bit puzzled. Last Thursday I met this girl. She was your very double. Do you have a sister working here at the supermarket?'

A high flush stained the girl's cheeks. 'Not here,' she said. She fiddled around and straightened her *Big Issues* in the bag. 'Thursday you say?'

'Yes. In the supermarket.'

The girl's hands fell to her side. 'Up till Monday, I had a sister. Now we hear on telephone that my sister dies on Monday. Three days before Thursday. A bombing.' She put her hand on her throat. 'My sister have a mark here. Like a fish.'

Esme looked at her. 'What has happened?' she thought. 'What has been happening to me?'

'I must go on,' said the girl. 'I must work.' Her soft mouth closed in a grim line. She picked up her *Big Issue* bag, fished out a copy and gave it to Esme, who opened her purse and extracted the fifty pounds with which she always set out in the town. The girl glanced around at the busy street. 'No. No.' she said. 'I cannot.'

Esme pressed the notes into her hand. 'Flowers for your sister. Truly!' Then she turned round and fled down the side street back to her own house, her own kitchen. And she cried. She cried for the *Big Issue* seller and her sister who had been killed in a bombing. It seemed that her whole body was melting and transforming itself to tears, running down her neck and into her shirt. After half an hour she washed her face at the sink, dried it with a tea towel and sat back down at the table. She opened out the *Big Issue*. The headline said something about peace talks in the Middle East.

The next Thursday, after an enjoyable time at the Costa knitting club, Esme went to the supermarket because she'd run out of fruit – very necessary for picnics. She filled her basket with plums, bananas and tangerines. There were only three people in the queue at the sixth checkout so she joined that queue. Her glance raked the length of the checkouts and stopped at the last one. The wooden panelled checkout was there again. The girl with the close headscarf was also there, smiling up at her customer as she registered his purchases. Esme's eyes moved to the man and she blinked. There was no doubt that it was Maurice, although his hair was spiky and more white than blond. And he was wearing a purple roll-neck sweater which he would always have despised as 'trendy'. And he was laughing with the girl, looking into her eyes. He could even have been flirting.

Esme was looking around wondering how she could make her way to that last checkout, when a boy cannoned into her, upsetting her trolley. He mumbled something and helped to put her trolley upright and gather up the scattered fruit. It took some minutes for Esme to reassure him that there was no harm done and to regain her place in the queue. Now, when she looked along the checkouts there was no wooden panelled checkout, no blond man, no girl with a close headscarf and seahorse birthmark.

Her head buzzed as she unloaded the trolley into the boot of her car. As she settled behind the wheel and put the car into gear, a smile spread across her face as big as the sun.

Support You Ever More
Ian Harris

IAN HARRIS is the father and grandfather of an ever-expanding family in the North of England. By day he is a factory machinist, by night he is a writer of fiction. He is an incurable hoarder, and has previously been published in the e-zine *Every Day Fiction*.

FIFTEEN MINUTES TO half-time, and at nil-nil there'd been little so far to warm the sparse crowd on a dull, grey, November afternoon. Lower league football can be as exciting as any, with players of lesser talent playing with passion and enthusiasm for the love of the game, rather than for the stratospheric wages of the pampered prima donnas at the very highest level. At least, that's what I insist when I find myself in some remote corner of the country in some crumbling, damp shed of a stadium on my ongoing quest to visit every league ground in the country. I try to convince myself that tense, thrilling encounters can be found in the most unlikely of places, and quite often I surprise myself by coming across an exciting match in the dullest of surroundings... this, sadly, was not one of those games. This was simply a mid-table, mid-season encounter between two groups of low-division cloggers, grimly hoofing the ball back and forth over a quagmire of mud. It was woeful.

That hadn't deterred one particularly loudmouthed supporter, however, from screaming his displeasure at every misplaced pass, mistimed tackle or misjudged refereeing decision, his bovine bellowings easily drowning the muted mutterings of the rest of the crowd. My only question was why, with so many vacant seats available all around the stadium, he'd chosen to sit directly behind me... I hunched down in my seat, huddled into my collar, and tried to ignore the lout.

The home team's striker received the ball in the penalty area with his back to goal. In a single, fluid movement he brought it under control, spun, and unleashed a blistering shot. The crown groaned as the ball flew high and wide, way over the crossbar, to disappear into the stands behind. The striker adopted the customary head-in-hands pose, then began trotting back to his own half.

The yob behind me leapt to his feet and unleashed a stream of profanities at the hapless centre forward. I flinched, partly at the volume of the shouting in my ear, but mainly in embarrassment because a couple of seats to my left sat a little lad, maybe eight or nine years old, who surely shouldn't have to be exposed to language like this. I gave him a surreptitious sideways glance. He didn't appear to be particularly bothered by the moron behind us; he was simply sitting there, his chin on his fists, seemingly engrossed in the game. His shoes were old-fashioned and well worn, his knitted bobble hat faded and unravelling at the edges.

Oddly, there didn't appear to be any adults with him; no one was interacting with him or paying him any attention so far as I could see. Who lets a kid this age go to a football match alone? I wondered. Maybe that was the done thing back in the Thirties or whatever; I remember my dad telling me stories of young boys being passed overhead by the adult fans down to the front where they could see the match, but those times were long past. Nowadays it's all stranger danger, keep the kids indoors on the Xbox, lock them away to keep them safe. I realised with a start that I was staring at this kid, and hurriedly turned my attention back to the pitch.

The game was bogged down in midfield, neither side making any particular progress forward. The referee had taken to whistling at the slightest infringement, breaking up the flow of the game, frustrating players and spectators alike. The idiot behind me was cursing again, promising dire consequences for the unfortunate arbiter unless he allowed the players to get on with it. I glanced at the little boy again.

He must have felt my gaze, because this time he turned his head and caught me looking at him.

The poor little soul looked frozen, and half starved. The flesh of his face was unhealthily pale, and dark shadows sat below eyes too young surely to hold such sadness. He wore a thin jacket that would have been out of fashion even in my day, over a jumper in his team's colours that had clearly been home-knitted.

It's never a good idea nowadays for a lone bloke to be caught staring at a strange child. I hurriedly did an embarrassed half-smile head-bob, and turned back to the match.

A home-team midfielder with the ball was attempting to dribble his way free through a mass of bodies in the centre circle. He almost succeeded, but then two of the opposition adeptly caught him in a double shoulder charge. The player went down with an audible hiss of escaping air.

The lout behind me reacted instantly, screaming obscenities at the offenders and vociferously exhorting the referee to halt the game and punish the miscreants. The referee, however, had seen nothing, and merely waved play on, which raised the yob to thus far unseen levels of rage. The torrent of bile which spewed from him was both disgusting and frightening. I was burning to turn around and confront the ignorant hooligan, to remind him that a child was present and to ask him to show some restraint, but, of course, at any football match that's a sure route to a swift punch in the mouth so instead I swallowed my anger and glanced with what I hoped was a sympathetic grimace at my diminutive neighbour to my left.

He was staring at me intently. Startled, I twitched my eyes briefly in the direction of the thug, and mouthed, 'Sorry about that. Don't pay any attention to him. Some people are just ignorant idiots.'

The boy's eyebrows shot up. He looked past my shoulder, then back at me, and shrugged. 'That's all right. I'm used to it.'

I nodded wisely. No doubt he was used to a lot of things, poor little soul, judging by the state of him. What sort of home life must he have? Who would let him out, let alone allow him to come to a football match unaccompanied, without at least giving him a feed and putting some clean clothes on him? Absent father, drunken mother, no doubt.

'Never seen you here before,' the thin voice piped.

I hesitated. This was getting uncomfortable. I didn't really want to get into a conversation with a child, here in a strange football ground far from my home town, but those oddly pale eyes were boring into me, expecting a reply.

'No, I, er, I've never been to this ground before,' I murmured, and left it at that. I glanced to my right, hoping no-one had noticed me talking to the child.

'You're not a supporter of the other team, though?' the boy persisted. I squirmed. Hadn't anyone ever warned this kid not to talk to strangers?

'I travel around a lot, for my job,' I explained in a low mutter. 'Whenever I have a few free hours, wherever I happen to be, I try to see the local football team. Actually, I'm well on my way to visiting every ground in the football league. It's become a bit of an obsession, to be honest.'

I was babbling too much, I realised, and smiled nervously. The little boy didn't smile back.

'I've only ever been here,' he said.

No surprise there.

We both turned to watch the match. Maybe now this seriously weird little kid, with his out-of-date clothes and his strange way of talking, sort of polite rather than with the cocky arrogance of most of today's kids, would leave me alone.

An opposition player had gone down under a strong tackle, and was writhing on the turf as if he'd had a limb severed. The loudmouth behind exploded in indignation as the referee waved a yellow card and the team physio came running onto the pitch, magic spray at the ready. A free kick was awarded and the player jumped to his feet, ready to continue the game.

'My Dad used to bring me. A long time ago, when I was small,' the child suddenly said. It seemed he wanted to talk for some reason, dammit. I reluctantly made an interested face.

'But I haven't seen him in ages, so now I just come on my own.'

Aha, thought so. His father had probably done a bunk when the responsibilities of fatherhood got too much. Or he'd been locked up for drugs. Something like that, anyway. That'd explain the tatty clothes and the waif-like appearance.

I was trying hard to keep my attention on the game, but the urge to inquire further soon won out. 'Doesn't your Mum worry about you, being here all on your own?' I asked.

He shrugged, and made no reply. So there was something he didn't want to talk about, anyway.

A thunderous bellow exploded from the seat behind me. On the pitch, the away team had managed, through an untidy goal mouth scramble, to bundle the ball into the home team's net. The referee's whistle signalled the goal, barely audible over the torrent of obscenities the yob was yelling. After the usual congratulatory knee-slides and pile up of bodies, the jubilant players of the away team went racing back to their positions while the home goalkeeper plucked the ball from the back of his net and dejectedly launched it towards the centre spot.

Eventually the loudmouth ran out of vulgarities to scream at the referee, the opposing players and even his own team, and the gush of invective slowed to a trickle.

'That was a shame,' the little boy said, quietly, 'I thought we had a real chance in this game. I hope we equalise soon.'

I was beginning to get seriously concerned for him. 'Why don't you sit somewhere else?' I suggested.

'No,' he replied, 'I sit here. I have to. This is my seat.'

'But you could sit anywhere you like,' I insisted. 'There's plenty of seats. You could get away from this moron here, anyway.'

'I have to sit here,' he repeated. 'This is my seat.'

I gave up. The whole situation was now too uncomfortable; this weird kid, insisting on chatting against all good sense, and the idiot behind, with his constant yelling and cursing. I couldn't stand it anymore. I decided to move.

'Look, it's nearly half time,' I suggested, 'I'm going to the burger van before the queue starts.' I was thinking I'd get out of this section of the ground and move to another side. Then looking at his gaunt little face, I almost found myself asking if I could get him anything. But then I realised that if the kid took me up on my offer, I'd have to bring it back and go on sitting here in front of the loudmouthed yob.

The boy nodded, and went on watching the match.

I stood and made to squeeze along the row toward the aisle. First though, risky though it was, I couldn't resist taking a peek at the lout who'd spent almost forty-five minutes roaring obscenities into my ear. I cautiously half-turned.

The row behind me was empty, as was the row behind that. Baffled and increasingly alarmed, I spun round and around, imagining that the yob had spotted me talking to the child and decided I was a dodgy character in need of a slap. I felt that at any moment a bear-like paw would be closing around my neck and a meaty fist would be crunching into my face.

There was no sign of anybody. Nothing.

'Where'd he go?' My voice was strangely high. I must have been beginning to panic. 'He was just here a moment ago. He was shouting, right there, a few seconds ago. That big-mouthed bloke! Where'd he go?'

The boy glanced toward the empty row of seats with a disinterested expression.

'He's been called back,' he said.

'What? Called back... What?'

'His time was up. He was called back. It always happens.'

'Called back? Called back where? What happens?'

The little boy looked right at me and his pale eyes pierced my soul.

'He used to come to every match. Always sat there, shouting and raging all through the game, really nasty stuff. Vile. Until one day his heart couldn't take any more, and a couple of minutes before half-time, it just burst. That was ages ago, of course, when I was small.'

'But what happened? The stewards would have given him CPR, wouldn't they? Got him to hospital?'

'It all happened so fast,' the child said.

'But...'

'So now he still comes to every match, still gets all worked up and shouts all those horrible things, though now it's usually only me that can hear him. Then when his time's up, two minutes before half time, just at the moment his heart stopped at that other game, he has to go back. They call him back.'

I looked from the empty seats, to this skinny little boy with the matter-of-fact expression on his face, who now turned unconcerned to watch the remaining moments of the first half, his chin resting on his fists. On the pitch, the referee was looking at his watch, gauging the minutes to half time.

I quickly shuffled along the rows towards the burger van.

Intruder
Kitty Fitzgerald

KITTY FITZGERALD has written five novels, including, *Pigtopia*, (Faber & Faber), which took second place in the Barnes & Noble Discover Awards for fiction. Her short stories, *Miranda's Shadow* were published by IRON Press in 2015. Several plays for BBC Radio 4 and for the stage. Her modern fable, *The Water Thief*, will be published in 2017 (IRON Press), with illustrations by Nicola Balfour. She has edited four anthologies of fiction for IRON Press most recently, *Root*. Her website is <www.kittyfitzgerald.com>

THE END OF term and it's been a tough week: drastic news, unusually hot weather and sleepless nights. Now you have six weeks before the Autumn term and the arrival of a new intake of eager students. The evening is too still, there's almost a pre-storm feel to it. You run a bath and tilt your head to catch the scent of the sandalwood oil. You've put a flask of cocoa, a tin of biscuits and a pile of magazines by your bed.

When the bath's ready, the main doorbell rings and you sigh. Will it be answered by anyone else in the building? It rings again. Outside your flat, footsteps tumble down the stairs. Tony from the top flat is going. The tension in your muscles eases as you melt into the water, turning so that every part of your body is drenched.

Dropping your head back, you allow the spicy liquid to flow around your chin until a subliminal warning scorches through your body. Someone's watching you. You swing your head towards the bathroom door. It's a stranger, a young man. The adrenalin rush sends you dizzy. You grip the sides of the bath.

'Hello,' he says, 'sorry if I startled you. I'll wait in here until you get out.'

He turns and walks out of sight. You squeeze your eyes in disbelief. You live alone, there's no bolt on the bathroom door and you must have left the hall door unlocked. You climb out of the bath and into your towelling dressing gown. You pause, search for the right words. He beats you to it. From the doorway, he says,

'I'm Terry, I know your sister, Carol. I just heard about your cancer and wanted to talk to you.'

You pull at the neck of your dressing gown. Terry holds up a bottle of wine.

'Corkscrew?' he asks and wanders towards your kitchen.

You stand there listening to him fumbling in drawers and clinking glasses. The sounds are muted by the white noise in your ears. You told your family and closest friends that you weren't yet ready to talk about the cancer. Carol wouldn't have gossiped with anyone.

You slip out of the bathroom door, slide along the wall and into the hall. The key isn't in the door. From behind you, he coughs. You turn, knowing he'll be dangling it in the air like some TV thriller character. Is there anyone in the house to hear you scream? You do it anyway.

'Waste of breath,' he says. 'The guy who let me in was on his way out and I checked the other flats.'

He has an overwrought sense of melodrama, watching you over his shoulder with the open wine bottle in one hand and two glasses in the other. His hands are tiny, delicate. You lurch forward, grab the sleeve of his sweatshirt; he's so thin you only catch the material, not any flesh or bone.

'What the hell are you doing in my flat?' you shout.

He shakes free, puts distance between you.

'I haven't come to sympathize I've come to give you advice.'

'Why would I take your advice? I don't know you.'

He puts the glasses on the coffee table and pours wine almost to the brim of each one. He's small in height too, a couple of inches shorter than you, dark hair, a thin mouth and child-size, even teeth.

'You look silly standing there,' he says.

You recall some police advice about not being aggressive in this sort of situation. You thought it was nonsense at the time but you'll give it a go. You sit in the chair farthest away from him.

'Please go. I don't want visitors tonight. We could meet sometime for coffee.'

'Would you turn up?'

You say nothing.

'I want to help you,' he says.

'You don't know me.'

'Carol talks about you all the time.'

'You don't know her.'

You stand and pace the room.

'Don't keep interrupting me,' he says.

The cold monotony of his voice offends you. You sit on another chair, one nearer the hall where you'll hear any footsteps on the stairs.

'I wasn't surprised to hear you'd got cancer. It's a symbol of imbalance; a disease people inflict on themselves. It's insidious.'

In spite of your anger, you want to laugh at his arrogance.

'You think you're superior, don't you?' he says. 'But you're punishing yourself because secretly, you know it's all a sham. You've fooled everyone with your pretence of confidence. But at night, in the dark, there's no getting away from it; each dismal thought feeds the cancer, helps it grow.'

He pushes his chin out, extends a thin, bony finger towards you. You jump in before he can speak.

'That's enough. You've had your stupid joke, now you can leave.'

Behind your back you cross your fingers.

He grins.

'Look at you, so wound up you don't know how to relax.'

Small studs of sweat turn cold on your neck. You recall the moment in the impersonal hospital room when the diagnosis was confirmed. Malignant, such an expressive word but not any business of this wretch who has prowled into your sanctuary.

'You're sick,' you tell him.

'You should listen to me.'

'I've no interest in what you have to say.'

You wonder if he's carrying a weapon.

'Doctors are in thrall to the global pharmaceutical industry. They get paid for prescribing. Why would drug companies want a cure for cancer? It makes them billions of pounds every year. Don't let them persuade you to have chemotherapy. Honestly, I know what I'm talking about.'

Your skin itches. Your sister, Carol works in the X Ray department at the General. Could he have met her there?

'You're scared of me aren't you?' he says.

You shake your head. You're uneasy, angry but not actually frightened. Perhaps you should be.

'I worked at the hospital and I got so angry one day, I punched a consultant. I was arrested and later, they sectioned me.'

'Why are you telling me all this?'

He shakes his head slowly but says nothing.

You stare at him, trying to work out what he wants. You want to get dressed but in some strange way that would normalize things. You notice he hasn't drunk any of the wine.

He stares at you and sticks his chin right out, like some cartoon character, then flops back heavily in the chair.

You decide to blank him out.

'Do you find me sexually attractive?' he asks.

You shake your head, unhappy about the turn in the conversation.

'Aren't I aggressive enough for you?'

'I'm not attracted to aggressive men.'

'What are you attracted to then?'

You sigh.

'Answer me. What are you attracted to?'

You imagine rusty crags, hills covered in mulberry heather, water tumbling down steep valleys. You think of films, books, theatre and music that you love. You remember wonderful people you know and have known. You recall making love on grass, in snow, in the rain and on the sand. But right now, you dream of perfect solitude.

'I'd like to be left alone,' you say.

His laughter is harsh. His hands relax their grip on the sofa cushions. He picks up the wine glass and puts it back down.

'Rubbish,' he snorts. 'Nobody likes being alone.'

'What do you want? Do you need to frighten someone to make yourself feel good?'

He leans forward, tapping his fist on the table for emphasis.

'You said I didn't scare you.'

You ignore him and turn away.

'I've had experts biting their nails to find labels for me: dominant mother syndrome, latent homosexual...you name it. What I want is respect. You look down your nose at me and you've no right.'

You walk closer to him, soften your voice and curb your anger.

'I have every right to choose my friends and who I invite into my home. Respect has to be earned.'

For a moment he appears to be listening. Then his eyes stray off into the distance and his fingers again start kneading the cushions. You shake your head, move away and lean on the kitchen doorframe.

'You really are sick,' he says. 'Humans are naturally sociable but you're antisocial and that's why you're punishing yourself. My problem is I'm too sociable and people like you don't like that, so I'm a threat. I am a threat.'

You're tempted to dash into the kitchen and grab a carving knife.

'Why do you want to be a threat?' you ask.

'Keep people on their toes.'

'If you're as sociable as you say, Terry, where are all your friends? Why are you spending Friday evening hassling me?'

He sits quite still, rapidly opening and closing his eyes. His breathing is shallow. You keep talking.

'Is there a reason why you've chosen me to upset?'

'Because you always ignore me.'

'I've never met you.'

He stands, wags his finger and sucks his lower lip.

'I've been in your company dozens of times.'

You close your eyes; try to conjure his face somewhere in your life before today. Sometimes, when you see people out of context it takes a while to recognise them but nothing clicks into place.

'I've sat around the next table to you at The Flower Pot pub on Busker's Nights. I've sat in the same row at the cinema.'

'Have we spoken to one another?' you ask, giving him another chance.

'You ignored me.'

He shivers, feels his face, looks down at his body, as if to reassure himself it's still there. You wonder if he has mental health issues and if he has, you're not sure if you have the energy or the experience to deal with them. He glances over his shoulder and at last it comes to you. He's your postman; did he open your hospital letter? You're usually at work when he delivers but a couple of weeks back he brought a parcel on a Saturday morning. As far as you can recall, that's the first and only time you've been face to face with him. You take a deep breath, stop leaning on the doorframe, take a few steps towards the hall and decide to rely on your wits.

'Can you hear that, Terry?' you ask.

He tries to focus on your face but he looks worn out.

'Time to go,' you say. 'That's my upstairs neighbour's car pulling into the drive.'

He stands up and walks to the window.

'You're lying,' he says. 'I'm disappointed, I thought you were better than that, Polly.'

For some inexplicable reason, this hurts. You feel like you've played your last card and rack your fuzzy brain for something else. And then, downstairs, the front door slams and a voice shouts up the stairs,

'Tony? Are you up there?'

It's Tony's girlfriend, Sarah. You and Terry stare at one another. You could scream but you don't. Something like a shadow passes across his eyes. Sarah's footsteps echo on the stairs. Terry takes your key out of his pocket, holds it in the air for a moment, and walks towards the hall.

Your head lightens a little. He stops halfway to the hall door, turns back to look at you.

'We could've known one another,' he says. 'I could have helped you.'

You don't reply. You're trying not to hold your breath. As Sarah's footsteps move past your landing, he goes to the door, puts the key in the lock, turns it, opens the door and walks out. You rush to the stairway and listen. You want to be sure he leaves the house. The front door opens and closes. You run to the window but there's no sign of him in the street.

You fight to get your breath back. He had no right to come into your life, uninvited and insist that he be known. On the coffee table the two full glasses of wine seem to stare at you.

For reassurance, you phone Carol, your sister. She answers almost immediately.

'Hi Polly.'

'Hey babes, listen, this might seem strange but do you know a guy called, Terry? Dark hair, small frame, tiny teeth and a bit psycho?'

She doesn't answer.

'Carol?'

'That's just so weird.'

'What is?'

'Why are you asking about him? You don't know him do you?'

'You do know him then?'

'Yes, he did voluntary work in our long-stay kid's unit for years until he got too ill. Why?'

'Because this evening he came to my flat, uninvited. Locked me in and virtually held me prisoner.'

The silence grows.

'Carol, why aren't you saying anything?'

'Are you sitting down?'

'Just talk.'

'Polly, Terry is dead...'

Your heart thrums against your ribcage.

'He had cancer. He didn't want to have chemotherapy but the doctors persuaded him. He only lasted for two weeks. He died at eight pm last night.'

How to be Invisible
Chris Barnham

CHRIS BARNHAM lives in London, a city which is a constant inspiration for those who want to write about unexpected problems from the future and dark secrets from the past, colliding with the present. Stories have appeared in places like *Compelling SF, Black Static* and the long-defunct *Pan Book of Horror*. His first novel, *Among the Living*, is available on Amazon, and his second, *Fifty One* is due out later this year from Filles Vertes Publishing. You can find him on Twitter: @barnham_chris and blogging about this and that at <www.chrisbarnhamwriter.wordpress.com>

ELLEN LEAVES EARLY on Saturday morning. She says, 'When I get back tomorrow you need to go.'

'I've got nowhere to stay.'

'You should have thought about that.'

Polly eats her breakfast cereal in silence. You have your laptop on the table, searching for places to stay. You make phone calls while Polly watches you, her eyes like dark holes.

There is a flat available in Manston Road, which isn't far away. You hold Polly's hand as you walk down the hill. Walking with her is like dragging a suitcase with no wheels, she leans backwards from every grudging step.

'Want to watch teevee,' she says.

It's a three-storey Victorian house backing onto the railway line. It isn't much, although better than some of the others in the street, which look empty and abandoned. A cracked window on the ground floor is held together with diagonal strips of tape, looking like someone has painted a cross to warn of plague. The landlord coughs repeatedly onto the back of his hand as he shows you the flat. A smoker's cough, like wet sandpaper. He smiles at Polly and tries to tickle her under the chin but she hides behind your legs.

You can see why the flat is available for rent immediately. There is peeling wallpaper and a smell of damp. A grey bloom of fungus clings to a leaking pipe beneath the toilet cistern.

'Who lives here?' Polly says, her words distorted around the thumb she won't stop sucking.

'I'm going to be staying here for a while.'

She stares at you, and then says: 'Does mummy know?'

It was the kind of thing that could happen to anyone, a silly mistake at the Christmas party. Sarah works in the next office to you. You never really spoke to her much before but she laughs at your jokes and lets you buy her more drinks. When you step outside for some air she follows you and lights a cigarette. You can't say who moves first, but you remember noticing how tiny she is when you kiss in the dark alleyway behind the pub. There is newspaper and discarded burger boxes around your feet and her mouth tastes of cigarettes. Her blouse is cut low and the shadow between her breasts is deep and dark.

'You're funny,' she says when you both move deeper into the privacy of the alley. 'I always liked you. I'm not the kind of girl who does this with just anyone.' She unzips your trousers and her head bobs low in front of you. Do you put your hand on her breast before that? You don't remember and it doesn't really matter.

These things happen. It's Christmas, when everyone is drunk on desperate good humour and terrified that their lives are rolling downhill too fast. It could end there, but you're stupid and you see her again. And again. Inevitably Ellen finds out just as Sarah refuses to see you anymore.

Polly is asleep when Ellen returns from her mother's house on Sunday evening. Ellen's eyes are dark with spent tears. There must once have been warmth in those eyes when she looked at you, but now they are pieces of ice mined from a deep underground lake. You leave with a shoulder bag containing your laptop, and two black bin liners stuffed with clothes.

In the street you see someone you know. Her name is Victoria. She's friendly with Ellen. She and her husband once came to dinner at your house. Or Ellen's house, as perhaps it is now. You wonder if she knows what has happened. You turn into a side street and run to the next corner to avoid being seen.

You go back to Ellen's house two days later. Ellen departs immediately to have dinner with a friend, and no doubt through their conversation to drip more poison into the ears of the neighbourhood, turning people against you. You give Polly fish fingers and sit with her while she watches television. You take her small hand in yours and her fingers grip yours tightly for a few minutes before she lets go and puts her thumb in her mouth.

You bath your daughter and read her a bedtime story. You tell her you'll see her again on Thursday. She quickly falls asleep and you sit in the kitchen until Ellen comes home and you leave without a word being spoken. All the way down the hill to Manston Road you feel an itch between your shoulder blades as if Ellen's stare leaves a scar.

At work you tell no one what has happened, but it is obvious everyone knows. Sarah looks through you as if you have become transparent and her friends duck into side offices when you walk down a corridor. You sit at a table in the staff canteen and conversation congeals into silence until one by one people pick up their trays and leave.

Your shame consumes you like acid. Occasionally you catch someone looking at you and the flesh melts from your bones. Next day you call in sick.

The man in the flat above yours is called Malcolm. You meet him at the front door on your third evening and he invites you in for a drink.

'Excuse the mess,' he says as he snatches underpants from the back of a chair, where they have been drying. 'Don't get many guests in.'

Malcolm is also separated from his wife, soon to be divorced, good riddance at last. When you sit down, the thin chair cushion exhales a wheezy cloud of dust.

You don't like whisky, which is all he has, but you drink it to be sociable. He gives you his only glass, while he drinks from a cup. You don't take long to get drunk, and as you do you become quieter. Malcolm is the opposite kind of drunk. He talks louder, telling you more than you want to know about his marriage break-up. It is a story that a million other men could tell but Malcolm recounts the tale as if convinced you will find it remarkable.

He was unfaithful, but his wife turned a blind eye until he lost his job, and then it was goodnight Vienna. Anyway, she had a boyfriend all along, the hypocrite.

'Never mind.' He swirls the whisky around the cup before draining it. 'Fuck her. Fuck the bitch.'

This prompts you to think about the last time you tried to fuck the bitch. The two of you hadn't been doing it much in recent months and Ellen didn't seem to mind. But the night after your lover dumped you, you drifted into lovemaking. Halfway through you started to cry and then you confessed.

You quickly get bored on your first day off sick. You find a box of dusty books in the bottom of the wardrobe. Most of them appear to be medical textbooks. Maybe a doctor lived here before.

One book is briefly interesting. It is about brain injuries. You read an article on a phenomenon called visual neglect. Apparently some people can suffer damage to their brain, perhaps from a stroke, which causes them to ignore objects on one side of their field of vision, despite having fully functioning eyesight. There are examples of people shaving only one side of the face, or ignoring food on one side of a plate, even though they complain of being hungry. Patients often collide with objects or structures on the side being neglected, such as door frames. It is as if things become invisible when you don't pay attention to them.

After a few days there is a message on your phone from work. You can't face calling back just yet, so you delete it.

You lose track of time. You don't go out much. You don't want to see anyone. One time, you are walking back home from the local shops, carrying bread and a tin of beans. Coming towards you, but on the opposite pavement, is a man you know. He is called Thomas. He has a son in Polly's nursery. You have been to the pub with him and another time he and his wife, a fat blonde woman called Debbie, came to your house for dinner. When you and Ellen were together.

You don't want to meet him. The thought of having to talk about what has happened places a chunk of cold lead in your chest, makes your head feel overstuffed and heavy. Maybe he will tell you what a failure you are as a father and a husband, and you will curl up in shame and blow away like dead leaves. Or, worse, he may be sympathetic, but you will both know how glad he is that you are down in your hole alone while he still has his wife and child and a life worth living.

There is no side street to turn into, no hidden doorway to shield you from view. It is too late to turn round and walk away in the opposite direction. Thomas is only twenty yards away. In seconds he will glance your way and he cannot fail to see you.

You stop moving, pressing yourself back against the side wall of a house. Your breath stills and a momentary bubble of silence englobes you. Thomas crosses the road to your side, glancing each way along the road to check for vehicles. He looks your way. You see his eyes move in slow motion, tracing a line across the street, sweeping along the pavement towards your feet, rising higher until he looks straight at you. You cannot remember when you last took a breath and you feel no need ever to take another. You feel yourself folding up – click click click – until you are too small to see.

And on his gaze goes, with no hint of recognition or interest, passing through you and further up the street. He walks slowly by, passing inches in front of you, so close you can smell the last cigarette on his breath.

'You can't keep coming here,' Ellen says one evening. It's two weeks after you left, so probably your fifth or sixth visit to oversee Polly's bedtime.

'But Polly...'

'You can take her to your place, if she wants to come. But I don't want you in my home anymore.'

'Can't we try to be grown-up about this?'

'You've got a nerve saying that, after what you did. Anyway, Polly's not that bothered whether you come or not. She says it's boring when you're here.'

In truth, it is painful to spend time with your daughter. You take her to the park and push her on the swing. When she looks at you, even as she laughs at the giddy height of the swing's pendulum motion, you feel a terrible weight of childish judgement. She doesn't yet know enough to despise you, but it is only a matter of time. As she grows older and Ellen fills her with bitterness, it is certain that Polly will blame you for the disappointments that life inevitably delivers.

You hold your daughter's hand as you walk her home from the park. Her small fingers are cool and dry and in a few minutes they slip from your grasp. When Ellen opens the door, Polly walks inside without a backward glance and no one speaks before Ellen slams the door and you walk away.

The days are very long. You take to walking to fill the time, leaving the flat in the morning, wandering aimlessly through urban streets. It has never been hard to go unnoticed in London and now you find it easier than ever. You avoid eye contact and keep your head down when people approach, keep your elbows in and fold yourself down into a narrow space. Occasionally you get lost, but you never ask directions. What if someone wanted to strike up a conversation, ask you things about yourself? It will not take them long to perceive your shame, to see you for the worthless person you are. You don't want to talk to anyone because you know that they will look in your eyes and see right down to the core of every useless thing you have done.

Instead you turn away, close your eyes, step sideways and slip from view. You are surprised how easy it is to be unnoticed, how comfortable it is to drift through the days with no expectations on you. Sometimes at home you sit in front of the chipped mirror on the wall and watch your reflection from the corner of your eye, trying to lose sight of yourself. It is painful to see your shame etched in the lines of your face and sometimes you can see the wall behind you, plainly visible through your fading head.

One day you look out of the window and see Ellen standing in the street, looking up at the house. She is alone and you wonder where your daughter is. Does she go to school now? Ellen looks straight up at the window where you stand. You raise a hand and sketch a wave, but she shows no sign of seeing you.

You could go downstairs and open the door, invite her in for a cup of tea, or go with her to the café up on the main road. You could talk to her; really talk, like two people with important things shared in their past. Maybe there is a way back.

You step back from the window and slip into shadows. When you look again at the street, Ellen has gone. Did she knock at the door? You don't recall. You make tea only for yourself. You can barely pick up the mug, unable to get a proper grip on the handle. You sit for a long time and stare at the table through your papery hands.

The leaves fall and the days get darker. Your clothes grow larger so that you have to make new holes in your belt to hold up your trousers. You like it this way; slipping deeper in among the folds of the garments so that less and less of you is visible.

You stay indoors more, only going out early in the morning or late at night, when few people are around. There is one time that you make the mistake of being out during the afternoon. You are on the pavement in front of the small local parade of shops, in plain view with no trees or bushes to conceal you. You hear a child's voice and see Polly, twenty yards away, running towards you with her arms spread wide. An open-mouthed smile of excitement glows across her face and fires a beam of electricity deep into your heart. Ellen walks a few paces behind her.

For an instant everything is frozen, suspended weightless beneath the blind sky. You might pretend that there is a chance of redemption. What if you reached out to swing Polly up in your arms? Hugged her tight to you again the way you did when she was born? Looking over the top of her head, you could catch Ellen's eye and maybe she would smile and the things that you broke could be mended.

To do that, you will have to step forward. You will have to be a different person. You will have to swallow your shame; suck it down and digest it.

You can't do that. Your shame has eaten better than you have in recent months and it has grown bigger than you. It surges up your throat and through your veins to your fingertips. You look down at your hands but you can't see them.

Polly giggles as she reaches you and runs past, so close you can smell the strawberry shampoo she loves. You turn your head and see her disappear into the sweet shop. You can't turn back to face Ellen. Her eyes will stop your heart. There is a high-pitched whistling noise all around as you step sideways and duck your head low. Your shabby coat slips up and over your face. You hold an arm in front of your eyes and through it you see your wife's legs walk past.

Maybe later you will go home. Later, when it is safe to move without being seen. Polly and Ellen come out of the shop and walk past you again.

Soon they are gone, leaving you alone to fade into the wind.

The Undertaker's Boy
Karen Turner

KAREN TURNER has taught English Literature in secondary schools and at the University of Hull, where she completed her PhD in nineteenth-century women's fiction. When not reading or writing she enjoys gardening and running, though not at the same time. She is currently working on a historical fiction novel.

I'LL SAY RIGHT at the outset, I don't believe in ghosts.

In my line of work, it would drive you mad if you were constantly looking over your shoulder for evidence of the dead rising up and exacting their revenge, or whatever it is they're supposed to do. Thirty years in the business and I've never seen the slightest shred of evidence that there's an afterlife. Assistants have come and gone over the years, many of them scared stiff – pardon the pun – by things they imagine they've seen or heard in the funeral parlour.

I'm far too rational to be influenced by all that, and I'm perfectly comfortable working alone when the assistants start fainting and departing in terror. The dead can't hurt you, unlike most of the living. There are plenty of very reputable undertakers out there who will swear the very opposite, that there is unquestionably an unseen world populated by spirits. I'm not one of them.

It was the school secretary who phoned me initially, to ask if I'd be willing to take on a temporary apprentice. A year ten boy, work experience, for a couple of weeks, she said. Just let him observe and follow you round, she said. I thought about it and agreed. An extra pair of hands around the place would be quite useful, and it's always good to bring fresh blood into the trade.

When the boy turned up on Monday morning, I was confronted by a pale, gangly youth who was all arms and legs. He was slightly built, with a shock of perfectly white hair and an owlish look. He had unusually long fingers, I noticed.

'Long fingers like that, made for playing the piano,' I remarked.

He flexed them and shrugged.

'I don't play the piano, Mr Barclay.'

His name was Adam, and he seemed polite, if rather reserved at first. I started him in the office with some paperwork. Just filing, answering the telephone, checking invoices. Simple, routine tasks. I asked him what had first attracted him to the undertaking business.

'Just thought it sounded interesting,' he said.

'You're not nervous about seeing dead bodies?' I said.

He shook his head.

When Mrs Hope was brought in, I wheeled her to the beauty parlour. It's not really a beauty parlour, just my way of talking. I think it sounds a bit more pleasing than 'embalming room'. She didn't look too bad already, so I thought she might be a good example for young Adam to see. She was an attractive woman in her late thirties, with thick honey-blonde hair and good bone structure.

'OK,' I said to him. 'We're going to make Mrs Hope here look even more beautiful than she already is.'

He stood quietly behind her head, watching me attentively.

I explained that we were going to pop some cotton wool inside her cheeks, to make her face look a bit plumper, and then we were going to give her a bit of a makeover. I pulled the little make-up trolley nearer and angled the light onto her face. I started to apply some of my tried and trusted 'Naturally Bronzed' foundation.

I noticed Adam tentatively working his fingertips against Mrs Hope's temples.

'She doesn't like foundation,' he said. 'She never wore it. She doesn't want cotton wool in her cheeks either.'

I chuckled.

'They all get the same treatment in here,' I said. 'The relatives want something pretty to look at. Let's put some blusher on her as well. Give her some colour in her cheeks. I'm also thinking maybe a touch of eyeliner and some mascara?'

'No,' said Adam. 'She doesn't want it.'

I put the brushes down and frowned at him.

'Perhaps you could save me some work, young man, and tell me what else she doesn't want.'

He closed his eyes and massaged the dead woman's temples with his long bony fingers.

'She doesn't mind being dead,' he said. He spoke slowly, choosing his words carefully. 'But she doesn't want to be turned into a circus. I think that's the word she used. She doesn't want people gawping at her, and she doesn't want all those colours on her face. She doesn't want to be touched. She just wants to lie in a casket and be buried.'

I gave him the kind of look that most people would recognise as irritation. He just opened his big owly eyes and blinked.

'I can't help what she says,' he said.

'You don't expect me to believe that you're actually communicating with a dead woman?' I said. 'I've been in this business longer than you've been alive, boy, and I can safely tell you that no dead person has ever spoken to me.'

'Maybe you never asked for their opinion,' he said.

'Damn right,' I said. 'What would be the use of that? What should I do, sit down in a darkened room with every corpse that comes in here, asking 'Is there anybody there'?' I waggled my fingers theatrically. 'I haven't got time for all that nonsense, for one thing. For another, a dead body has no consciousness. It can't talk to you.'

'Don't refer to her as 'it',' he protested. 'She doesn't like it. And she doesn't like you shouting.'

'I'm not shouting,' I said.

'You do sound a bit tetchy,' he said calmly. 'And a little disrespectful.'

'I've had about enough of this,' I said. 'I tell you what, why don't we have a little look at some of our other clients, and you can tell me what they think too.'

I jerked my thumb towards the door and he quietly got up and followed. I led him first to the relatives' room, where a wicker casket was awaiting collection. The occupant was a man in his fifties who had suffered a thrombosis. I had been rather proud of this one. When he came in, his face was sunken and his complexion sallow, and I'd managed to plump him up nicely and get him looking much more sanguine. Adam said he looked like a pantomime dame and rubbed some of the blusher off with a tissue.

He put his hands on the corpse's head and said I shouldn't have used embalming fluid because the gentleman was anxious that his remains should break down as quickly and as naturally as possible. He was looking forward to his green burial, and to experiencing genuine connection with the landscape. He hoped that someone would plant bluebells on his grave.

I checked in the files and found that most of this information was not far off. I had failed to notice the instruction not to embalm, and the burial plot was booked for the new site on the outskirts of the city. I don't know how the boy could possibly have known, but I imagine you could have guessed most of it from the eco-warrior casket. Where he got the thing about the bluebells from, I don't know.

Next I took him to the chapel room, where he found that the late Maria Corvaggio had already made some tentative excursions to visit her family, and had frightened the life out of her sister by appearing at the top of the stairs in a black veil. She had made a telephone call to her cousin in Italy but had found herself unable to speak so she had hissed and crackled instead. She was now looking forward to her funeral and was planning to pull the organist's hair during the recital of Bach's Toccata and Fugue in D Minor. It was a piece of music that she particularly disliked but which had been chosen for her by a well-meaning relative. She was also planning to pull the heads off all the white lilies that had been ordered for her.

The lad had some imagination, I'll give him that. I decided in the end he was harmless enough, just a bit odd. I asked him if he had many friends. He said, 'No, not many.' I advised him to think about writing as a career. Or maybe stand-up comedy.

We returned to Mrs Hope in the beauty parlour. My intention was to send the lad for lunch, and then get her face done while he was out. In the meantime we had to prepare her casket.

I decided I would humour him. While I was cutting the white satin lining, I asked him about his affinity with the dead, and how he came to realise that the dead could apparently speak to him.

'I dunno,' he said, after a thoughtful pause. 'I guess that being dead doesn't mean you suddenly have no feelings. You live your whole life with a head full of thoughts and memories, and when you stop breathing those thoughts and memories and feelings must go somewhere. Mr Connor told us in Physics that you can't destroy energy, you can only change it into a different form. I think dead people are still there, just in a different form and in a slightly different place that not everyone can get to.'

'Maybe you should be a medium,' I said. 'Plenty of people charge money for that kind of thing.'

'Charlatans,' he said derisively. 'Cold readers, exploiting the vulnerable. Death is only hard for the people left behind. It's OK for the dead.'

'But, surely,' I said, 'if everyone who ever died is still here, there'd be no more room for the rest of us.'

'They're not supposed to *stay* here,' said Adam. 'Once they realise they're dead, they know they have to go somewhere else.'

'Heaven,' I suggested.

'Something like that,' he agreed.

The casket was ready just before midday, and we carefully lifted Mrs Hope to rest in the relative comfort of padded satin.

I left Adam there with her while I went to the office to check on the paperwork, just to make sure there were no outstanding requirements from the family. I was thinking about the embalming fluid mishap and didn't want to make any more mistakes.

The office has a large plate glass window from which you can see the entrance to the treatment rooms. While looking through the computer files, I thought I saw a movement out of the corner of my eye and glanced up. I saw Adam and Mrs Hope calmly walking hand-in-hand out of the beauty parlour, and down the corridor. They paused, turned to look at me over their shoulders and waved before they walked out through the front door. I saw them. As real as anyone else. Not transparent, or shimmering, or see-through. Real, solid-looking people. My hands were shaking, and my heart was hammering so hard that I felt slightly faint. I steadied myself against the door frame and lurched to the beauty parlour. There was Mrs Hope, lying in the casket, looking serene and utterly peaceful, and Adam was nowhere to be seen.

I ran to the front door, looked up and down the street, then I checked every room in the building. He was nowhere.

I phoned the school.

'I'm calling about the work experience boy,' I said, when the secretary answered.

'Oh, I'm so sorry, Mr Barclay, I meant to phone you this morning. You'll be wondering where he is. I'm afraid he had a slight problem with transport and should be with you just after lunch. I'm very sorry, it won't happen again.'

'No, wait,' I said, confused. 'I mean the work experience boy who turned up this morning. Adam.'

'Adam?' she said, sounding equally confused. 'No, the boy we're sending is Michael Harvey.'

'Then who's Adam?' I said. 'Thin, spooky looking boy, about 5' 8'. White hair. Big eyes. Odd.'

There was a brief silence and a slight intake of breath.

'How did you know about Adam, Mr Barclay?'

'That's what I'm trying to tell you,' I said, glad we seemed to be getting somewhere at last. 'He was the work experience boy, and he's just disappeared. Literally. He was doing fine. He was a bit strange, but he seemed to be handling everything, and he just walked out a few minutes ago. Not a goodbye, or thanks for having me, or anything.'

There was another silence.

'Mr Barclay, the boy you described sounds very like Adam Hope, who was a pupil here. He died a couple of months ago in a cycling accident. His mother passed away last week. He was such a lovely boy...'

The hairs on the back of my neck were standing on end and I had goose bumps all over. There was something shaky going on in my stomach.

A boy who was dead had apparently come to my funeral parlour to collect his mother, who was also dead, and both of them had just walked out. I saw it with my own eyes, I know that. But I don't believe in ghosts.

Playing In Their Own Time

Tracy Fahey

TRACY FAHEY writes short fiction concerned with folklore, the domestic and the uncanny. Her short fiction collection, *The Unheimlich Manoeuvre*, was published by Boo Books in 2016 and her work has appeared in thirteen US and UK anthologies. In 2016 two of her short stories were long listed by Ellen Datlow for Honourable Mentions in *The Best Horror of the Year Volume 8*. <www.designingtracy.wixsite.com/tracyfahey>.

IT'S TWO IN the morning when we hear the voices, a crackle of static, a faint burst of sound that dies away almost at once. I start and catch our soundman's arm.

'Did you hear that?' I mouth at him. He nods, eyes distant, head to one side, carefully listening. I swallow, my heart beating light and fast in my chest, and wait to hear if there's more. I inhale a long suck of air that smells of cold stone and damp floors. Seconds tick by, invisible and loud. I strain my ears into the aching, waiting silence. The soundman lifts one finger to alert me, and then presses it to his lips. There is nothing but the drumming in my ears…and then I hear it. A small voice says 'Play', so quietly and faintly I am frozen, breathless. I see a zig-zag of green dance up and down on the computer screen. Our tech guy replays the burst of sound on his headphones, I see the blip dance again. He gives me the thumbs up.

We got it! I am torn between fear and glee.

John Farrell puts on the headphones and listens intently. I watch his thick eyebrows knit together as the first sound traces its seismic thread across the screen. He makes to take off the headphones. I circle my hand urgently in the air to signal that there's more to come. He relaxes back on his chair, only to sit forward sharply again.

'That's her!' His headphones are on the table, his face ablaze with eagerness. 'That's the same girl I hear!'

'Good.' I draw in a deep, satisfied breath, the long, cold night, and the ache in my back all forgotten. 'Do you think you would be ready to do a rough interview with us?'

Transcript of first interview. August 20th 2015

Jonas:	*In Ballinagh Castle, owner John Farrell has been experiencing some disruptions. He called us in to investigate. So we packed our bags, our cameras, our electronic voice recorders, our lighting, our computers, and most importantly [laughs] our crew, and left to spend what would surely be an unforgettable night there. John, can you tell us about the history of the castle?*
Farrell:	*Well, emm, the castle's been in my family since it was built. Originally the family were the O'Farrells and they were chieftains here in Limerick. But over the years, the family was ousted by the Anglo-Irish and there was a family here, name of Mercer, who occupied it for a few generations. But no luck came to them, the lands were cursed, it's said, by the O'Farrell's, so the crops failed, the beasts died, even the family started to die out. And then it reverted back to us – the Farrells – we were Farrells by then – until it fell down in the 1960s.*
Jonas:	*That's where you came in.*
Farrell:	*Right enough. I'd always had an interest in the place, and when it came up for sale in the early 1990s, I got it for next to nothing. No real roof, only a wing left habitable, but it was always going to be a work in progress.*
Jonas:	*But almost as soon as you moved in, you had some strange experiences.*
Farrell:	*I did [clears throat]. We all did, my wife, my daughter, myself.*

	Strange things. Like the sound of doors closing where there were no doors. Like voices talking together, but like an old BBC broadcast, old-fashioned voices, and only for a few seconds each time. Of course, there was never anyone there. Apart from that, there were a few odd things that were more visible. There was a chair that you'd find overturned in the main hall, for some reason, and windows that would be opened when you thought you'd closed them... [pauses]
Jonas:	*[encouragingly] And there was one manifestation in particular?*
Farrell:	*Oh yes, of course, the little girl. [voice softens] A lovely little thing, you'd catch a glimpse of her from time to time in the upstairs gallery. Just a little thing in a white dress, you'd see the material flutter out of the corner of your eye. But if you looked at her full on, you'd lose her, she'd just go indistinct and fade out, like a bad TV signal.*
Unknown:	*[in background] We can slap a shot of the gallery over that.*
Jonas:	*Fascinating. Tell us more about her.*
Farrell:	*Well, I don't really know much more. She's a little girl, we think maybe she's the last of the Mercers? Her dress seems very old fashioned, at least Victorian. There was a poor mite who fell down the stone stairs in the mid-eighteenth century, the only child of the house. My wife has seen her more than myself, and she says she's heard her playing around upstairs when we're down here at night.*
Jonas:	*And even your daughter's seen her?*
Farrell:	*Deirdre? She has indeed. She's not scared in the least [laughs]. When she was little she was always plaguing me, wanting to play with her. Now she's turned seven, she doesn't do it so much anymore. But back then she'd cry and chase around the gallery after the girl, and I had to explain it to her, that the castle was full of people, but all locked in their own time. We can see and hear them, sometimes, like an echo, but they're lost in the past, they can't see further than their own time-span.*

Jonas:	*Fascinating hypothesis. Do you feel these spirits are in any way malignant?*
Farrell:	*I don't. We're very comfortable with them. Them in their time, us in ours. They're more like a radio broadcast from another era. Harmless.*
Jonas:	*Thank you John for that insight into life among the ghosts of Ballinagh Castle. But we wanted to find out for ourselves. So we set up our equipment and prepared ourselves for a long night, waiting, listening… [trails off]*
Unknown:	*[in background] And fade into the shots of the set-up.*

[transcript ends]

We're upstairs in the gallery, packing up the gear in the cold wintry light of the afternoon, coiling up cables, dismantling the installation. I put away my notebook in my satchel, then stick my hands under my warm armpits and wiggle the numb fingers around in an attempt to recover some feeling.

'God, it's cold.'

'Imagine living here.' It's Matt, one of the lighting guys. He's blowing on his hands.

'It's fine,' says a small voice beside us. We both start, and then laugh. Standing beside us is a small girl. It's Deirdre, John Farrell's daughter. I recognise her from the photographs in the Great Hall. She scowls at us, obviously insulted by our casual denigration of her home. Matt smiles at her apologetically and moves off to pack up the lighting equipment.

'It's not so cold,' she insists. 'I play in here all the time.' Deirdre has a cute, cross little face, sprinkled with freckles. I drop to one knee beside her.

'You've seen the girl in here?' I ask. Strictly speaking I shouldn't, John was quite adamant he would be the spokesperson for his family, but my curiosity is too great. Her face is scornful.

'Yes, of course,' she says. 'I see her all the time. And I hear her.'

'What does she say?'

She stares at me with her clear blue eyes for a moment. 'She wants to play. She always wants to play. But she can't see me.'

'What does she look like?'

Deirdre's blue gaze doesn't falter. 'Look behind you. She's there.'

I whip around, rattled, and see...nothing. At least I *think* it's nothing. My heart is beating too quickly. Deirdre turns and her footsteps clatter lightly down the stone steps. There's a sudden wriggle of shadows in the corner under the mezzanine. Faintly I hear it, the merest breath of a giggle that hangs in the air. I don't hesitate. I turn and run after her, my steps huge and blundering, all the way back into the Great Hall.

Years later, I've almost forgotten Ballinagh Castle. We're at the dreaded Monday staff meeting, the slowest hour of the week, when we get together and 'throw ideas around' as Peter calls it. Peter is a good decade younger than me, with a luxuriant, lumberjack beard and hair greased and parted carefully on his narrow head. He's a terrible human being. He is also our boss.

'Didn't you film the original episode at Ballinagh Castle?' Peter points at me, pistol fashion. I nod.

'Right, so, for the new series we're revisiting the most popular locations over the last six series – Ballinagh always tops the polls – we cover what's happened since our visit, any further manifestations, blah, blah.' He clicks his fingers. 'And of course we'll intersperse the new recording with the original footage. Only half the filming needed!' he smiles broadly around the table.

Idiot, I think automatically, as I do every Monday morning. But this is a special kind of stupid, even for Peter. The real expense of any shoot is transporting equipment, crew, the elaborate set-up, the time-consuming take down. None of these equate to the exact minutes of edited film produced. I say nothing and try to suppress an eye-roll at Matt who is now our senior technical officer. Since Amy came, I've discovered real fear, the scary abyss of potential job loss when you have a little person who relies on you utterly. Consequently, I've tried to bite back smart remarks and to become more subdued, less argumentative.

After the staff meeting, it's a tradition that Matt and I have our own staff meeting in the local coffee shop, where we allegedly draw up new plans based on the previous meeting, but where we *actually* compete to parody Peter's latest bright idea over an Irish breakfast.

'Back to Ballinagh, then,' says Matt, forking a strip of bacon into his mouth. 'That was the spookiest place we went to – definitely the oddest place in that series, if not in all the series we've filmed.' He chews solemnly. 'You even had a weird moment there, and you're a hard-core sceptic.'

I draw in a breath, remembering that moving shadow, that giggle, as if it were yesterday. 'Yeah. There was something there alright. So should I ring ahead and book a slot? I reckon if we get started on that one it'll get Peter off our backs.'

Matt nods, absorbed in cutting his sausages into neat, bite-sized chunks. Then he looks up.

'Hang on, before you do, I've just remembered I heard something. There's something that happened there.' There is a note of urgency in his voice. He pauses and sets down his knife and fork. 'It happened a few years after we were there.'

I look at him, puzzled. 'Like what?'

'Like some kind of tragedy.' His face is knotted in near-recollection, and then he waves a dismissive hand, and instead thumbs out a Google search.

'Ach,' he says. 'Oh no.'

'What is it?'

'That poor wee girl.' Matt's Belfast accent is stronger when he's upset. 'That wee girl Deirdre. She died.'

I catch my breath, her freckled, grumpy face clear and vivid in my memory. 'Jesus, that's awful. What happened? Are the family still there?'

'She fell, it seems. Poor girl.' Matt's face is soft with pity as he reads off his phone screen. 'And yes, they're still there. His name is still on the contact page of the castle website. God love him.'

All I can do is nod. The feelings this evokes are dark, overwhelming. I am caught in an intense pang of sadness and an almost simultaneous guilty throb of relief that it wasn't me, wasn't Amy.

'Ah the luxury of TV travel in Ireland,' says Matt, stretching out in the limited space of our van cab. 'Other paranormal investigators on wealthy US programmes get massive black shiny jeeps; we get a couple of shabby vans with 'Irish Mysteries of the Paranormal' inscribed in faded letters on the side. (The rest of the presenters call us the Imps. Ha ha. We're used to it.)

'A little more cramped than usual,' I say apologetically. 'I have to go by Joanne's house to collect Amy.'

'Bringing a kid to a haunted house?' Matt looks perplexed.

'Look, you know Joanne. It's her weekend away, so she's being totally adamant about it. If I don't stick to the arrangement, she'll do that passive-aggressive thing of 'forgetting' arrangements or booking Amy in for activities on my time…' my voice trails off, as I remember the succession of complicated peace treaties negotiated after Amy's birth.

Matt nods. 'Ah, I know,' he says easily. 'It's fine by me. As long as you don't expect me to babysit.'

John is there to welcome us, just like the last time. I'm shocked at how much he's aged; his thick hair and wiry moustache are white. Strong lines have dug themselves into the thick flesh of his forehead, and carved deep runnels either side of his mouth. He smiles when he sees us, but it's a quick, fleeting grimace.

'Welcome back,' he says, stepping back from the door. I follow him inside as Matt and the crew start to back up the vans.

'I'm so sorry,' I say, quick and embarrassed, moving in to shake his hand. He returns my grip, but weakly. I persevere. 'I would have been in touch earlier, but I just heard.'

He looks up. 'You met her, didn't you? Little Deirdre.'

'Yes.' I can barely look at him. The glint of tears in his eyes makes me feel like bawling. I think of Amy in the car, and again I feel that same, sick, churning mixture of grief and relief.

He shakes his head, as if to clear his thoughts and silently motions to me to follow him inside.

Inside the door, in the former Great Hall, everything is more cluttered than I remember. Slow, classical music plays from an ancient record player in the corner. Thick, furred dust covers the heaps of newspapers piled up behind the door. The bookcases are even fuller, the books lining them two and three deep, but they too are white with wood-smoke dust.

The cut firewood seems to be the only recent addition to the room, and the crackle and spit from the fireplace is the only cheerful sound in it.

'Daddy?'

It's Amy, standing just inside the door. Matt must have let her out of the van. She shrinks back a little from the strange house, and the strange man inside it.

John's head shoots up, and he smiles. A real smile this time, pure with pleasure. He cocks his head at me.

'Is this your own little one?'

'Amy.' I supply.

'Come here to me, Amy, and say hello!' John opens his arms and, to my surprise, Amy, bashful little Amy, whose phrase of the moment is a piteous 'I'm SHY', simply runs forward. She opens her chubby arms wide, her full weight falling against him with the happy, heart-breaking confidence of a child.

'Well aren't you just fabulous?' says John, giving her a tight hug. 'Have you come to see me?'

'Yes,' says Amy, smiling up at him. 'Do you have any toys? And sweets?'

John grins. 'I have apples out the back on the trees. Is that OK with your Daddy?'

I nod, relieved. Amy stands with her tummy stuck out, considering the offer.

'FOUR apples,' she pronounces.

'One,' I correct her, with mock severity, and watch her skip off with John.

It's later, much later. Amy is asleep on a pull-out bed that John has made up by the side of the fire. She sleeps on her tummy, one arm thrown above her head. From time to time she makes a small, muttering sound that lapses back into wavelets of serene breathing. Matt and the crew are manning the rooms upstairs, as John and I talk by the crackling fire in the great hearth.

'So you stayed here?' I ask. I don't add the word 'afterwards', though it hangs in the air like an unspoken thought.

He dips his head, watching a glowing coal roll slowly down the stack of burning wood beneath. 'A place like this. It's hard to leave. My wife Grainne did, though. She couldn't take it, you know, the perpetual reminder. It's hard. It's all hard. Having a family, loving them, losing them.'

'It is.' I feel impelled to share my own story, if only to dilute the awfulness of John's. 'Amy's mother, Joanne, we were never really together. It just happened, and she wanted nothing to do with me. I had to argue my way into being part of Amy's life. I see her every weekend, but I'm always afraid that Joanne will go for sole custody. And I live in dread of being sent on weekend shoots.'

'Like this one?'

'This one's fine. You were very good to make her so welcome. Other shoots would be more difficult, in among ruins, or inaccessible spaces.' My voice trails off. I hear the self-pitying tone in my voice and am miserably conscious of my own relative good fortune. There is a silence as we both stare into the fire, hypnotised by the soft hissing of the frail wood as it burns down to dust and smoke. There's only a lamp pooling soft light beside the stairs, for the crew to get up and down.

'Calling Seb Jonas.' Matt's voice crackles through my earpiece.

'Here' I say, automatically moving away from the fire, voice dropped so as not to wake Amy.

'It's cold as hell up here. Not a peep out of anything. But I guess this time we're really listening out for the little girl, right? It's the logical hook to connect with the last episode and the recent tragedy.'

I steal a glance at John, hunched over in his tattered velvet chair. 'Yes,' I say quietly, feeling wretched. 'That's the important one.'

It's an hour later, and I'm just on the verge of sleep, in a cycle of small motions, where my eyelids continuously droop, fall, then start open again.

'Listen.' John whispers the word quietly. I open my eyes fully and sit up straight in my chair. The fire is dying down in the glowing grate and his face is cast in deep shadow. I see him raise a finger to his lips.

'Hush,' he breathes. 'She's back.'

'The little Victorian girl?' I whisper. *I hope Matt's catching this.* John leans towards me. His eyes close in a blink to signify *yes*, and then he settles back. His eyes travel over and back around the open door to the stairs. I feel a crawling sense of cold travel downwards, like a giant stone breath exhaled down the dark passageway. Amy is still sleeping. I watch John's gaze play around the corner of the room, and I'm suddenly afraid, with the sick kind of crawling, out-of-body horror that I've only experienced once or twice in my life. Then John sits forward abruptly.

'There she is.'

I strain my eyes, but all I can see is a flicker, a jump, a squiggle of shadow, so fast it's almost invisible. The best way to describe it is like a flaw in an old VHS tape – an abrupt burst of darkness that disrupts the screen. I watch intently for a few seconds, then look away – and there it is! A wave of movement, right at the edge of my vision, a flicker from another space, superimposed onto ours.

'She's there, all right, in her long white frock.' John is speaking softly, almost to himself. 'There she is, playing away. Don't be scared, she can't see you.' I feel cold dots of gooseflesh stipple themselves on my arms; I see them raised on my wrists. Then I hear a long, slow exhale beside me.

'And here she is. My own little girl.'

His eyes glint with heavy, trembling tears, and all at once, there is such a look of love and grief on his face I have to turn away. Tears roll down his craggy face, sparkling into funnels either side of his moustache. I move closer, and put an arm around his shoulders. I feel my own treacherous, hot tears rise, as his eyes travel back and forward across the floor.

'It brings me such comfort,' he whispers, rough breath catching in his throat. 'Such comfort.'

A coal falls in the fire with a thump. We both start; it breaks the spell. I am cold, terrified. I act on instinct, and pick up the sleeping Amy, holding her tight, so tight, her warm body folded into mine, her shallow breathing on my neck. I glance across. John's head is buried in his hands, gnarled fingers working convulsively through his thick white hair.

'That's why I don't leave,' he says quietly. 'Not while she's still here. Grainne didn't understand it. In the end she hated me for it. But I can't leave. As long as she's here, so am I…'

I feel the moth-soft flutter of Amy's eyelashes stir against my neck.

'They're still parted, you know.' His voice is gentle, almost hypnotic.

'They're in the same space, but playing in their own time. But now that they're both in that space…sometimes they can see each other. Sometimes I see them wave.'

My arms are trembling. I hold Amy, feeling her sleep-heavy body slip slightly against me. She murmurs, and I bend to catch her words.

'They want to play.' Her breath is milk-sweet and soft against my face.

As Amy lies, warm and heavy against my chest, I know absolutely what real terror is; that precise moment when you feel everything sure and certain and warm in your life start to slip away.

Sunday Lunch
Jenny Cozens

JENNY COZENS was born in Oxford, grew up in Australia and has lived in the north of England since 1970. As a clinical psychologist she worked in universities and the NHS, focusing on the causes of depression, the health of doctors and patient safety. As Jenny Firth-Cozens she's written various academic books but moved to more popular works in the 1980s, initially for newspapers and magazines, and later as agony aunt for *Good Housekeeping* and *The Yorkshire Post*.

THEY LAY DOWN their knives. They seem to do it almost in unison, but perhaps they're led by Louise. She smiles weakly at her sons to indicate that enough is enough, even if it does upset their grandmother to see food left. The uncooked bits of chicken glow luridly pink despite the care they've taken to push the meat under the mashed potato, to hide things as well as they can. Hiding things comes naturally. That way it seems to work.

Louise's mother tightens her lips but doesn't speak: Mary thinks that children should be made to eat everything. It saves the starving children in Africa. The words radiate from her in the silence. She hates fussy eaters.

It's only four o'clock but it's almost dark and the room is getting cold. They'd arrived late for lunch, as they always do. John, her daughter's uncommunicative husband, pours more wine, filling his glass and dribbling the rest into his wife's. He does it smoothly, smiling at his sons, barely glancing at the bottle. As if we don't notice what he's doing, thinks his mother-in-law, when really he's drunk almost the whole bottle and nearly all the one before. Mary puts on her glasses and looks at the clock: two hours still before their taxi will arrive. There is silence and it has to be filled.

'Well', says Mary to her grandsons. 'You seem to have had enough.' The potato now is stained crimson. 'Shall we play a game?' The boys look at each other and then at their mother.

'Do you have Cluedo grandma?' asks Matt, the elder of the two. His father will play Cluedo sometimes.

'I don't. You ask me that every time you come. There's cards. We could play snap. Or rummy even? You like that.' She watches their eyes connect again; an eyebrow raised and Louise's lips tighten.

'A séance', says John suddenly, as if he's just been startled awake by a loud command.

'A séance? Really?' The grandmother feels a quiver of excitement. It's been a long time since she took part in one of those. At a party when they'd all had too many Babychams and some girl wanted to know who she would marry. Who was that? Reddish brown hair, pulled into a ponytail. She remembers the amazement as the glass seemed to move. The quiver of fear that ran around the table. Was there an answer? There was certainly something spelled out but she can't remember what. It must have been thirty years ago or more, certainly before her daughter married this drunken man. Long before Mary lost Ron, her own wonderful husband, to a double-decker bus that leapt up onto the pavement where he stood with all his usual absent-minded patience. A dreamer, her Ron, but even a dreamer can be missed. He might just be waiting, patient still, hoping for the chance to return to her, to say sorry or tell her what it's like over there. Mary's getting old and she's starting to wonder about things like that.

Louise looks doubtful, as do the boys. 'Is it a game?' asks Matt.

'A great game,' John smiles. That settles it.

'I know how to do it!' says the grandmother and she's glad to see they look surprised. She goes to bring paper and scissors (blunt ones for the boys) from the room she calls the office, dark like this one. In mourning almost. They cut small lopsided squares and write a large, black capital letter on each one with felt-tip pens. The whole twenty-six, she tells them. And a square for YES and another for NO, this time in red. John watches them, smoking. How dare he, thinks Mary, as she always does. She passes him a delicate hand-painted saucer for his ash, just to make a point.

'Do you believe this crap?' he asks her daughter as Mary lays the letters alphabetically around the table, with YES on one side, NO on the other, neatly. Why did he suggest it if really he only wants to smirk, Mary wonders, but she notices that Louise doesn't even bother to answer him. Good. She hobbles to the cupboard to choose a glass – the thin-stemmed one Ron had liked for his beloved Gewurtztraminer that he insisted on each Christmas. He didn't insist on much and he'd appreciate that. It's the last one, left over from a set of six they'd bought in Swanage on their honeymoon. She turns it over and places it in the centre of the table. That will call him if anything will.

'What's going to happen?' asks the younger boy.

'Nothing,' says his father. 'Just something to amuse the girls. Girls' stuff!' And he widens bloodshot eyes in pretended horror. The boys glance at their mother and look down, each wondering which camp he should join, whether he should smile or not.

'You suggested it', says Louise and they see the white spot she gets on her cheek when she's cross. But it's small.

'I like amusing women,' smiles John. His mother-in-law knows that these words have a special married-couple's meaning – two meanings really – but she's long ago ceased to understand either of them. When they speak together now they do it fast, rat-a-tat-tat, running words together, their own secret language, and she can never follow. She knows very well she's not meant to and she's tired of trying.

'Put one finger on the base of the glass,' she tells her grandsons, and she lays her own there to show them how it's done. 'Just lightly. No one must push it. It goes on its own.'

They sit around the table, arms outstretched towards its centre, fingers resting obediently upon the glass. Nothing happens.

'I think we're supposed to say something', says the grandmother. 'Ask if anyone is there. Something like that.'

'Is anybody there?' asks John, using his very spooky voice, sing-song and quavering. The boys smile at him. He can be fun when he's drunk.

Nothing happens. They sit silently waiting. Come on Ron, thinks Mary. I want to talk to you.

'Is anybody there?' asks Louise in her ordinary school-teacher voice. The glass shifts half an inch to the left.

'You pushed it!' says Matt to his brother.

'No I didn't.'

'Did you push it dad?'

John screws his nose up and sniffs. 'It'll be your mother.'

'Is there anybody there?' asks his wife again.

Now the glass seems to jolt into life, haphazardly, jerkily. It travels to a B and hovers, glides to NO, shivers near the middle.

'Stop pushing it', says John.

'I'm not,' they squeak, almost in unison.

The glass begins to move fast, spinning between letters, seeming to hover long enough to read and then spinning on. The letters make no words. It's nonsense. It slides to the centre and seems to vibrate. Mary feels irritated, even ashamed. If it's Ron, he should do better. He used to be a good speller.

'I've had enough', says John suddenly, and he takes his finger from the glass and glares at it. At once the glass starts to move with purpose: 'J', it says; 'M'.

'It's for you dad,' shouts Mark. 'JM – John Murray. That's you!'

Mary is disappointed. She was sure that Ron would speak to her. She takes her finger from the glass. Now it's flying between the letters – JMJMJM. A very excited glass, pleased it's done something right.

'Who's there?' asks Louise.

John is standing behind his son, frowning, his face tightened with something that looks like fear. 'It's rubbish,' he says. 'You're pushing it Louise. Just stop it. You'll scare the kids. Stop!' He's shouting now.

The boys are wide-eyed. This is a new version of their father and, as they watch him, it gets worse: he starts to cry. Angry, impatient, reluctant tears. They've never seen him cry before.

'Do you know my mother's maiden name?' he asks Louise between sobs, spitting the words out as if he's accusing her of something.

'Of course not. She died long before I met you.'

'Ask it to go to the letter her maiden name starts with', he orders. The boys take their fingers off the glass. They don't like this game. It's not fun at all. Now only Louise is making contact but they can see that, as her finger slips from time to time, the glass still moves perfectly well on its own. They can see that, but can they believe it? Matt takes his father's hand and squeezes it.

'What does your maiden name start with?' mutters Louise to the glass, looking embarrassed at the stupidity of all this.

The glass travels slowly to A and then B and then C. As it wanders round the circle it seems to look hard at each letter before moving on. M, N, O, P. It doesn't know the answer, thinks the grandmother. It's all just nonsense. Q, R, S. Very disappointing. But then, at T, the glass quivers, slides slightly back and then shoots the T off the table. A single harsh, grating sob rips out of John and he turns and walks quickly from the room. Louise takes her finger off the glass, eyebrows raised.

'I thought it might be Ron,' sighs the grandmother. 'Your grandfather', she tells the boys. 'It's his favourite glass.'

'So is it him?' Matt asks.

'No. He was a very good speller. Not like this one. '

'No,' says John coming back into the room. He's wiped away the tears and his voice sounds angry. He's smoking again. 'It's my mother. Annie Taylor. Your other gran. It's how she was before she died. She'd had a stroke. She could only speak the first letter of words. We couldn't understand anything. It was horrible. It was just like that.' His voice is breaking again. Mark reaches over to take his father's hand.

'So she's still in that state, even though she's been dead so long?' asks the grandmother. 'Surely not.'

He laughs, but they can see he doesn't think it's funny. 'Not much to look forward to, eh Mary?' She shivers. She'd wanted something very different to this. She watches her daughter put her finger back on the glass, a lazy, absent-minded movement. The glass made her do that, Mary thinks, and knows that she is right.

The glass has started to move once more in a slow, thoughtful manner, travelling out from the centre and round the letters. All their eyes are on it now; they are believers, everyone of them converted. All at once, making the boys and Mary jump, the glass moves with a new certainty: straight to the V, then the I, back to the X, over to the E, and round to the N. Back to the middle, where it spins round so fast that Louise has to take her finger from it, but it keeps spinning anyway. VIXEN.

'Vixen?' says Louise. 'What does that mean?'

'What's a vixen?' asks the younger son.

'A lady fox, Dumbo,' says his brother. 'Isn't that right dad?' His father, ashen-faced now, doesn't answer. 'Dad? Isn't that right? Didn't you say that, when that lady came round? When mum was away? The one you work with at the bank. Dad...?' His voice is becoming a wail. No one is behaving the way he expects.

'What lady?' asks Louise.

'You weren't there,' says her son and all at once he knows this matters, matters a lot; that for some reason he shouldn't be saying it, but he needs them to recognize that his memory is valid. They need to believe him.

'She was pretty,' says his brother. 'I remember her too. She had red toenails.'

'Do I know her?' His mother's eyes are glinting and the white spot is large now, a splinter of shiny ice.

'You said her name meant vixen in old English. You both laughed.'

'I bet they did,' says Louise. Mark smiles at her, unsure but grateful that she at least seems to believe him. She doesn't smile back. 'So, John, your dead mother appears to be in on your activities. Seems to be there even if I'm not. Doesn't think much of it.' Now she smiles, but it's one of those bright curved tooth-filled lines she puts on when she's really angry.

'Am I missing something?' asks the grandmother, putting the glass in the sink with the rest of their dinner things.

'I doubt it,' murmurs John. 'Can we go home now? Talk about this later? Doesn't seem fair to the kids.'

'As you always say when it's convenient to you,' says Louise.

'I wish it was Ron', the grandmother whispers. 'It's my house. It should have been Ron.' She picks up the letters one by one and piles them neatly at the end of the table. 'I wanted to know things', she thinks. 'About that bus and what he was doing there and why that woman said he just stepped out. It's my house. She had no right barging in like that. It should have been Ron.'

Outside, the taxi's horn blasts out. Time to go. Mary takes the glass from the soapy water to dry it but the stem is snapped. No one has remembered to say goodbye.

Dulce et Decorum
Christine D. Goodwin

CHRISTINE D. GOODWIN is the proud mum of Paul, Dorothy and Billy, a Northumbrian Piper, Linguist, Teacher, Language School Director, Aspiring Writer, Translator, Photographer, Bus Pass Holder, Ukulele Player, Dire Straits Fan, Newcastle United Supporter, Blue Badge Tour Guide.

WAYNE AND SHAUN feared nothing, neither the darkness nor the dead. The moss covered stone monuments that glistened in the moonlight, the rustling of long grass and the sudden hoot of an owl held no terrors for them. They lived for the moment and cared not a jot for the dead. They lived for night-time moments spent swilling cans of cheap cider and fixing with heroin or any other drugs they could lay their hands on, when it was especially fun to climb up to the secluded and disused Hilltop Cemetery and enjoy their revels undisturbed.

You would have had difficulty in telling them apart, Wayne and Shaun, because they wore the same grey hoodies, the same grey tracksuit bottoms and trainers. Their heads were shaven. They spoke the same and walked with the same swagger. You would have to look very closely at their necks to tell them apart. Slithering up Wayne's neck was a snake, its head whispering evil into his ear and its red and yellow body spiralling around and down his left arm. Shaun's neck sported no tattoo but on the knuckles of his left hand, the word 'Mam' was written in crude capital letters. Wayne had always thought he was soft as shite, ever since they were kids when Shaun tried to stop him throwing the cat out of his bedroom window.

Shaun worked in the local recycling plant. His mother had been a single parent, now re-married to a lout who beat her occasionally. As for Wayne, he always joked that he'd attended a private school endorsed by royalty; detained at Her Majesty's pleasure in young offenders' institutions in other words. Wayne had laughed heartily and gleefully at the cat's wail and its twisted efforts to land on its feet. Shaun had laughed too, but it was a hollow laugh.

Hilltop Cemetery was a good place for outsiders like Wayne and Shaun. It was on the edge of town, the town where life appeared to be lived by the insiders, normal people going about their business – working, cooking, eating, drinking, playing in the parks, making love, having children, caring for their families, taking the kids to school, shopping in town, holidaying in Spain, sleeping soundly. Wayne and Shaun had no part in that kind of life so they shunned it. They lived in the dark. They lived in the night. In Hilltop Cemetery.

So it was that they came up to the graveyard one cold and dark autumnal evening with their plastic bags full of cans and supplies. Wayne had stolen money from an old lady. He'd jostled her as she opened her garden gate and grabbed her purse from her basket as she lay on the path, hurt and sobbing, pleading. He'd emptied her purse of her pension, just collected, and then threw it back at her, as if leaving her bus pass was an act of kindness. He'd bought cannabis and ketamine. It was going to be a good night in Hilltop Cemetery.

Wayne and Shaun started with the cider, and as they drank, nestled down in the long grass around the gravestones, they talked about football and girls, and bragged about their exploits, the girls they'd had, the crimes they'd committed, their best trips, their worst trips. Scattered all around them was the evidence of previous visits: no flowers for the dead, just empty beer bottles and cans, crisp packets, cigarette packets, syringes.

As they drank and smoked, Wayne laughed about the old lady, 'When she fell I could see her baggy drawers.' Shaun cursed his step-father, and his mother for marrying him. 'Bastard. The neighbours think Mam's clumsy. She keeps walking into doors.' They felt funny and witty and lay back to watch the mists rising from the earth and swirl around the gravestones and black clouds scudding across the full moon, blotting out the light and then slowly revealing it again. Before them stood the stone angel, her hands together in prayer and her face, half covered in moss, bent down staring at them in sadness.

'Time for some fun', said Wayne, and brought out the ketamine. Carefully laying the powder in lines on the top of his tobacco tin, he snorted, watched by Shaun and the angel.

'What's it like?' Shaun asked.

'It's cool,' said Wayne, 'Try some.'

There wasn't much left but Shaun spent time mixing the powder with tobacco and rolling a joint.

As he smoked, Wayne grabbed a beer bottle and hurled it at the angel's head. He missed.

'Target practice!' he screamed, pleased with his own good idea.

He staggered to his feet and for five minutes they both laughed and giggled as they stumbled around taking turns to smash empty beer bottles on the angel's head. She continued to stare peacefully at them, in constant sorrow and grief.

Suddenly Wayne's laughter ceased, his breathing grew heavy, his face reddened and anger erupted. 'I'm going to knock the fucking bitch down,' he screeched, overestimating his own powers, and began to push and shove with all his might at the immovable monument. When his efforts failed, he started kicking furiously at the angel. 'Lay off, man,' said Shaun, 'you'll break your bloody foot.' .

'Fucking stones. Fucking, fucking stupid fucking stones', cried Wayne, his face red with rage and tears forming in his eyes. 'Fucking bitch!' he snarled, kicking the angel one last time before turning on smaller less monumental stones. 'Fucking gravestones', he cried and began furiously kicking and pushing the headstones round about him. So off they both went, running amok through the graveyard, throwing stones and bottles at headstones, pushing them, knocking them over if they could. The wind rustled the grass and blew the clouds from the face of the moon, lighting up their graveyard spree as they destroyed the monuments to the dead.

There was no stopping Wayne. He disappeared into the darkness, on his personal vendetta against death. Shaun, not sharing Wayne's anger, leant on a headstone to regain his breath and try to control the thudding of his heart. He could hear Wayne's rampage, his shouting, cursing and swearing and the smashing of stones through the mist.

Then all of a sudden there was silence. The wind dropped. Black clouds covered the moon.

Darkness descended.

Shaun, alone, called out as he picked his way in blackness through the cemetery.

'Wayne, stop fooling around, man.'

'Wayne, where are you?'

'Wayne, where the fuck are you, man?'

He stumbled his way back to where they'd left their gear and found the torch. He could barely use his hands, fumbled to switch it on, tripped and lurched on his search for Wayne, his panic and fear growing, fed by the eerie silence.

He thought he was calling Wayne's name but then didn't know whether the sound had come out of his mouth. The torchlight picked out a skull carved on a gravestone and scared him half to death. It came towards him, closer and closer. He couldn't feel his feet. As he passed, the skull jumped out at him, he tried to scream but no sound came. He ran for his life and it felt that he was running on air. As he flew through the thick grass and the brambles, the beam of his torch found Wayne.

He was kneeling, staring up at something, his face pale.

Shaun stopped, shocked at the strange scene. He directed the beam at whatever Wayne was looking at but could see nothing. All he could hear was the sound of his own heavy breathing and his heart racing in his chest. As he watched, the wind got up again, the moon shone again, lighting up a swirling mist which seemed to rise from the ground like a shimmering cloud. A strange sweet peppery scent filled the air.

As he watched, Wayne's mouth seemed to open in a scream, his eyes popping out of his face. But the scream stayed in his throat. Wayne, who wasn't afraid of anything, was now helpless, unable to move, looking up at unknown terrors. He began blubbing, pleading. Tears were running down his face and snot was streaming out of his nose.

'Don't kill me!' he sobbed.

'I'm going to die, I'm dying, I'm dying, I can't move. Help. Don't kill me. I'm choking. Choking. Can't breathe.'

'Bad trip, bad trip, he's in the k-hole,' Shaun slurred as he tried to explain the situation to himself, 'Gorra gerrim outa here.' He lurched forwards, and despite the feeling that he had superhuman strength, struggled to haul Wayne to his feet. The peppery mist made him cough, but he dragged Wayne through the graveyard, down the hill and towards the lights of the town. All the way to his digs, Wayne was coughing and blubbering. 'Don't leave me, don't let me die.' But Shaun could do nothing for him other than heave him onto his bed and hope he'd sleep it off. Then, shaken and exhausted, he made his own way home.

The following day the police arrived. He was being taken in for questioning concerning vandalism at the Hilltop Cemetery.

'You fucking idiot,' shouted his mother as they took him away, and clipped him across the head as he left, 'What the hell have you been up to now?' Shaun said nothing.

Wayne and Shaun were both charged with criminal damage and possession of illegal drugs. There was plenty of evidence and their fingerprints were all over the paraphernalia they'd left behind.

A week later Wayne became ill. First it was the itching, then blisters all over his body. The blisters blocked his airways. He lay choking, gargling, drowning, his eyes desperate and writhing in his face. And the snake at his ear like a devil, sick with sin, became bloated with sores. He was taken to hospital, but despite all efforts, the doctors couldn't save him. It took him five weeks to die an agonising death. At the inquest, the pathologist said that he was mystified about the cause of Wayne's illness, that it may possibly have been caused by drug abuse, depending on what mixture of drugs had been used, but that if he hadn't known better, he could have sworn it was identical to the effects of mustard gas in the Great War.

Shaun spent some time at a Young Offender Institution and on his release worked for several weeks on community service, tidying and clearing Hilltop Cemetery, collecting the rubbish, cutting the grass and brambles, watched over by his supervisor, Mr Armstrong.

The work brought him one day to the spot where he had found Wayne. It was completely overgrown with long thick grass, weeds and brambles.

'You've got your work cut out there, lad,' said Mr Armstrong.

The memories of that night flooded into his brain and Shaun did his best to shake off the horrors by working as hard as he could. He worked feverishly, cutting down brambles, chopping, pulling, digging out roots, labouring until his body ached and until he came upon three little white gravestones standing in a row.

He knelt before them, and as he worked with fork and trowel to pull out the couch grass and dandelions, the smell of the earth and torn grass mingled with a faint peppery smell, a sweet scent. Shaun looked up to see above him three figures standing rigidly to attention. As he watched, transfixed, unable to work out what he was looking at, one of the figures stepped forward and pointed a rifle at his head. With a start, he tried to move but his whole body was suddenly leaden and he stared, transfixed. The figures had big black holes where their eyes should be, tubes coming out of their faces where their noses should be. But they were like humans. They were like soldiers. They carried rifles with bayonets fixed. And the rifles were pointing straight at Shaun. He fell backwards in shock, crawling away.

'Get up lad and get back to work'. His supervisor, Mr Armstrong, thought he'd tripped.

'No lying down on the job!' he laughed.

Slowly, Shaun picked himself up. He dared not move.

Mr Armstrong yelled, sergeant-major style, 'Get on with it, lad.'

Shaun stammered. Caught between fear of Mr Armstrong and terror of the rifle trained directly on him, he had little choice. He started, 'But, but...'

But knew there would be no explaining, that he would not be believed.

'No buts, Shaun,' said Mr Armstrong, watching like a hawk as Shaun picked up his trowel and dropped to his knees before the little gravestones.

Mr Armstrong, a hard task-master with a kind heart, was used to being vigilant for signs of drug abuse in the young folk placed under his wing and noted Shaun's odd behaviour, saw how he began to work frantically and feverishly, noticed the urgency of his labouring and his growing agitation.

Coming closer, he heard Shaun's heavy breathing and saw the pallor of Shaun's skin and the sweat dripping from his brow. Standing beside him, he saw the trembling hands and heard the quiet sobbing. And he smelt a faint peppery scent in the air.

Was it drugs? Or perhaps working too hard in the cold? And what was that smell? Was it Shaun's aftershave? He hadn't noticed him smoking anything. Mr Armstrong had a decision to make.

'Look, son. You've done a good job here. You'd better get off home now. Take some lemon and honey for that chill.'

Shaun stood up slowly.

'Thank you Mr Armstrong', his voice was almost a whisper.

Then he turned and addressed the air, his scream losing its power as his breath failed him and tears choked his throat. 'I'm sorry. Do you hear? I'm fucking sorry!'

Sobbing, he flung his trowel aside and ran as fast as his legs would carry him away from the rifles, the graves and Mr Armstrong, away down the hill towards the safety of the hustle and bustle of the town, where, amongst people going about their normal business, the busy high street would enfold him in its arms and soothe his fears.

Had he looked back, Shaun would have seen Mr Armstrong standing there, scratching his head in puzzlement; he would have seen the ghostly figures shouldering arms, and the three of them, in unison, as if responding to some unheard order, executing a perfect right turn and marching away into nothingness. But hurtling downhill, through the now peaceful, neat and tidy graveyard, he saw nothing, not even the little stone angel, who continued to bow her head in sorrow as he passed.

Had he been more observant, Shaun might have noticed that the three little headstones marked Commonwealth War graves.

Private Frederick William Jones of the 9th Battalion of the York and Lancaster Cavalry Regiment. Died 29th July 1918 aged 28.

Lance Corporal Arthur Ernest Hunter of 28 Sunderland Street, Cavalry

Division of the Durham Light Infantry. Died 5th March 1919 aged 24 years.

Private James Drummond of the Durham Light Infantry. Died 12th October 1917 aged 19 years.

Mr Armstrong, a keen local historian, did some research on the graves and discovered that Private Drummond had been wounded in France and sent to St. Thomas' hospital in London. He died, not of his wounds, but of the effects of mustard gas poison, and his body was sent home to be buried at Hilltop Cemetery five days later.

Wayne's family name was Drummond.

The Installation
Noreen Rees

NOREEN REES is a graduate of the MA in Creative Writing at Northumbria University. Noreen won the People's Play Award in 2001 with *Bloodlines*. Four further plays performed including *Not Some Kind of Sideshow* (Northumberland Theatre Company); two children's books – *The Picnic Tea* (Nelson Story Chest) and *The Beach Tree* (Northumbria University Press). Her short stories have been published in various anthologies and she has worked as a writer on community projects for several organisations.

A GUY WAS standing at my door holding a large brown box.

He was quite short, dressed in a navy fleece, work trousers and a navy beanie hat.

'Mr Lovecat?' he said.

'Sorry?'

'Mr Lovecat, your 'Cloud Extra' Freeview package. I've come to install it.'

'Right...er...OK.'

I hadn't ordered a 'Cloud Extra' package, nor was I called Mr Lovecat. The whole thing sounded dodgy. Yet he did have an ID badge.

'So..er where would you like it installed?'

I hesitated slightly then motioned to the lounge. He stepped into it, ignoring the pizza cartons and empty cans of lager on the coffee table. Actually I was glad to see someone. Anyone.

He carefully picked his way round the photo frame that was lying on the floor surrounded by shards of glass.

'Can you sign here please?' he asked.

'Well, er...'

'It's just to confirm that this is your address.'

I was warming to this idea. After all, he wanted to install a 'Cloud Extra' package and I didn't have one. And I did live at the address on his form, even if my name wasn't Lovecat. We were both winners. So I signed *J Lovecat*.

He began to unwrap the 'Cloud Extra' box from its armour of polystyrene, placing the components on the floor like an Egyptologist laying out a mummy's bones.

'You paid for the extra installation and set-up deal. I was expecting an older person,' he said.

'Oh, I'm really busy, wouldn't know where to start. Anyway, you're the expert.'

He seemed to like this and was soon attaching cables to sockets. I left him to it, went into the kitchen to try to find teabags and milk. The teabags were in the cupboard above the dishwasher. The organic porridge, herbal tea and rice cakes were no longer there. *She'd* cleared them all before she'd gone, three weeks ago. Since then I'd used the same plate to eat off and the dishwasher had become a sort of shrine, untouched and pure.

I opened the fridge. Yep, there was milk but it was lumpy and cheesy. I slung it in the bin but now it stank. So I lifted the bin bag out, and the cans of lager rattled against the numerous beer bottles.

'Sorry we're out of milk, mate,' I said, carrying two mugs of tea back into the lounge.

'No problem,' the engineer said, standing up and grasping one of the mug handles. I wondered who he lived with, whether he had a partner that cooked, and bought milk; whether he had children who hung on to his legs when he came home after a day of installing.

'Nice place you got here,' he said. That was probably in his script. I looked around at the CDs spilling over the floor, the dust on the bookshelf, the Sunday papers fanning over the settee. He put his mug down on the table. When he lifted it to drink there was a watery ring mark. *She* used to hover with coasters when people came. Now my few visitors marked their stay by a ring mark on the table, like the concentric circles on tree stumps. To date there were only three marks.

'It's unrecognisable round here now, this area,' the engineer continued.

'Yes,' I said as we drank the milkless tea.

'I was born and brought up here.'

'Oh, when was that?' I asked.

He didn't answer the question, only stared at his tea then said, 'They've knocked everything down, even my old school. The iron railings are still there, though.' He looked into the mid distance for a few seconds then said decisively, 'Right. I just need to complete my timesheet then you need to sign to say I've completed the work.'

He jabbed away with a stylus on an electric gizmo. It gave off strange sounds like whale music, as if there was some sort of interference on it.

'In no time you and the missus'll be watching the latest films and sport,' he said.

'It'll be just me, actually. I live here alone.' I felt as if I was in an AA meeting confessing to going on a three night binge. Maybe he was being diplomatic but he carried on prodding the device while it responded by making discordant bleeps. He passed it over for me to sign. Oh the bitter irony – Mr Lovecat with no one to love.

The engineer handed me a thick, glossy brochure. 'Your instructions, mate. My number's on there. Give me a call if you're stuck.'

Then he was away, out of my door, out of my life. Or so I thought. So I spent the evening reading the instruction manual. Eventually at five to midnight I finally got to watch an old repeat of *The Sopranos*.

What else to watch though? Ciara had taken charge of the remote when we moved in together. If I showed an interest in a particular programme, she'd sigh and pick up a fashion magazine. Lately though she'd put them aside for magazines with babies on the cover. Did she think I was that stupid? We were happy as we were weren't we?

A few nights after the unexpected Freeview delivery, the door-bell rang. Could it? But of course it wasn't her. She had a key. It was Mr 'Cloud Extra.' I didn't recognise him at first, partly because he was wearing jeans and a black quilted jacket. When I looked at him properly I realised that he wasn't the middle-aged bald guy he'd seemed to be at first. For a start his eyes were distinctive – a sort of Aegean Sea colour. He also looked a bit Mediterranean – Spanish maybe – but his accent was English. And he seemed to be slimmer, somehow. But I definitely recognised his voice.

'Er, unofficial call but I just wondered how you were getting on.'

'Fine, no probs.'

'Good, I'm glad about that.'

He seemed reluctant to go, hovered on the doorstep.

'The instruction manual was very good. Tell your bosses.'

'I will.'

He began walking away – a sort of sliding motion like a skater, almost as if his feet weren't touching the ground. And suddenly I felt in need of human company. Since Ciara had left I'd only spoken to my work colleagues at school, and the kids I'm a learning mentor to. I'd spoken to the cashier at the Spar Shop. Otherwise zilch.

'Come in mate,' I said. 'I've got some milk today.'

He sat on the sofa while I made tea. After his last call I'd bought a bag of one hundred and sixty teabags. I'd even bought some chocolate digestives. It felt almost liberating to pile the chocolate digestives on a plate, like an Aztec sacrifice. For the next hour I talked football with Mr 'Cloud Extra' AKA Sam, and we covered topics such as snooker, rugby, the cost of going to the gym. We compared notes on girls we'd seen in *Nuts,* though I got the feeling that Sam's girls weren't real, that he was just agreeing with me. Sam even told me he'd once marinaded something. But what we didn't talk about was why I was currently single.

Until the end that was.

'Well thanks for dropping by, Sam,' I said. 'You don't fix relationships do you?' I was only half joking.

'Wish I did, mate. I'd have a job for life.'

'I'm sure you realised...well, my girlfriend...'

'She just left? I had a feeling.'

This guy's intuitive, almost a mind reader I thought.

I picked up the smashed photo frame where it had lain untouched for three weeks. Tiny pieces of shattered glass fell onto the floor like crystals. Sam looked at the photo. Ciara and I were sitting on a Spanish promenade squinting at the sun.

'I never thought we'd break up.'

'It happens. Look if you don't want to talk about it –'

'No, that's it. I do but, well I'm going to sound like Billy No Mates here. I don't have anyone I can say this to.'

Sam leaned forward. For one awful moment I thought he has going to pat my shoulder but the hand hovered then found its way onto the armrest.

'I never saw the signs,' I began.

Afterwards I felt great. Talking to Sam had seemed so easy. But I realised I'd been blinkered and blind to what had been going on around me. I'd messed up completely, and from Ciara's point of view I wasn't really committed to the relationship. I could see that now, but it didn't look likely she'd give me another chance.

Sam patted my shoulder now. It felt good.

'I don't think I gave you my card.' he said. He laid a small white rectangle on the table. 'I have to go. You'll be all right now.'

'Yes,' I said. 'Thanks.'

And somehow I knew I *would* be all right. Life after Ciara would go on, and who knows, I might find someone else. And this time I wouldn't make the same mistakes. Sam slid out of the door. He didn't look back. Soon he was absorbed into the darkness beyond the street lamps.

Feeling buoyed up I switched on the TV. Man U were playing Barca in the European league. I watched Man U's players zipping around the field like red pinballs. I opened a can of lager. It gave a satisfying hiss as I raised it to my lips. Then the TV went blank. Completely. Zilch. I fiddled with the controls. Nothing. Then I tried to follow the instructions in the manual. I checked plug sockets, connections, even fuses but the only image I could receive appeared to be a blizzard in Antarctica. Then out of the snow came a faint message. *Welcome to Cloud Extra* it said.

I picked up the phone and rang the helpline number for at least twenty minutes. Eventually the call was passed to a human.

'Mr Lovejoy?' he said. I could hear the tapping of keys.

'I can't get any sort of signal on my set. Sam installed it.'

'Ah, yes, Sam.' There was a pause, and I could hear another voice in the background.

'Unfortunately Sam has now left the company,' the human said. 'Another engineer can call tomorrow, if that's convenient.'

It would have to do.

'So, there's a problem with Sam right?' I said. 'But he was only here today.'

'Unfortunately there was a problem. We can only apologise. He wasn't working with the authorisation of 'Cloud Extra.' You're welcome to keep the 'Cloud Extra' box in recompense.'

'OK, thanks. Can I just ask, why did Sam leave?'

'I'm sorry but under Data Protection I cannot give that information.'

'He was so helpful.'

'Yes. Our customers have said –' There was an electronic clicking then the line went dead.

I had a sudden urge to contact Sam, to hear his side of the story. I felt angry on his behalf. Why had they sacked him? But maybe they hadn't. I rang the number on his business card. There was some strange mood music but there didn't seem to be a way of leaving a message.

The next night the engineer arrived as planned. He was young, lanky, didn't seem to have time to chat.

'No I haven't heard of anyone called Sam in our engineers' team. There was a guy a while ago, before my time, but I think something happened to him.'

'What happened?'

'Some accident I think. But like I say that was before my time. Well, that's your problem fixed. Just sign here please.'

Once again I wrote *J Lovecat.*

A few days later I was channel hopping, trying to choose between *World Darts* and *Countdown* when the remote button jammed. The channel I was now viewing seemed to be one of those cheap-as-chips shows comprising CCTV camera images. But there were no car crashes or dodgy sales people. It was a shopping mall. I jabbed at the remote. Nothing changed. But then, there on the screen was a guy in a familiar black quilted jacket. It was almost as if he'd just materialised, like someone being teleported in a Star Trek episode. It couldn't be Sam, surely? Then he came up close to the camera and gave a thumbs up sign. Suddenly the image was gone, and the screen was showing *World Darts*. I tried to get Sam back – tried for ages – but no luck. Maybe it hadn't been him after all. But the way he'd looked, the thumbs up sign, it just all seemed to make sense. I remembered what he'd said when we'd talked. 'You'll be all right now.' And just then the phone rang, and it was Ciara.

A Trick of the Light
Andrew Jones

ANDREW JONES is a retired solicitor. He was born in the North East and has spent his life in the region. He has recently begun to write occasional short stories and poems, mainly for his own amusement. After years of having to weigh every word in letters and reports written on behalf of his clients, he says it's a huge relief to be able to just make stuff up and admit it.

I WAS IN the kitchen when I first saw it; a flicker of movement at the window, which my eyes interpreted as someone having just passed by on their way to the front door. I had the impression that the figure I had just missed seeing was a woman's: tall, and with a straight back, like my sister Alex. I waited for her to come in, but there was no-one there. I thought no more about it, and it may have happened two or three times before I began to pay attention. It became a regular occurrence; I decided that it was a trick of the light, refracted through the old, irregular panes of the kitchen window.

The house was old; a plain, stone and slate, Dales cottage, it stood by itself on the outskirts of the village, well below the road, within the crook of a long, sweeping curve. It was invisible from a car; to see it you had to stop and look over the wall, which people often did in the spring and summer, when the banks rising up behind the house were bright with daffodils and later, flowering trees.

I'd moved there with my parents almost on a whim; we'd seen it and fallen in love with it and its garden. The ground floor windows looked out over a stone terrace with a rose bed below, then a lawn sloping down to the stream, which emerged from a culvert under the road. Anyone coming to the house by car would park at the foot of the drive then walk along the terrace to the front door, which opened into a lobby beside the kitchen.

Time passed; we settled in. Our old cat, who had passed most of her life in a series of small suburban gardens, decided, after one determined attempt to walk home, that she liked her new, expanded horizons. The winters were hard, and the frost seemed to settle in the air around the house at the foot of the banks that surrounded it, but its thick stone walls kept the cold at bay. When the thaw came the stream, usually gentle, would leap from the mouth of the culvert with a thunder that could be felt through the ground. In the summer a dipper patrolled the stream and a heron was an occasional visitor; and, once, a mallard took up brief residence, with her ducklings following her in single file through the garden. Below the house the stream flowed through a wood; our next door neighbours were the rooks, whose cawing was the background to our days, and who sometimes could be heard scolding and grumbling if we switched the outdoor lights on late at night.

After a lifetime at sea my father took to being in the country and enjoyed his daily walk, sometimes to the pub, where he became known as 'the Captain'. Then we discovered that he was seriously ill; suddenly our decision to move so far from the city seemed rash. I almost ceased to notice the flicker of movement that still tugged at the corner of my eye from time to time as I passed through the kitchen.

Spring came late that year; but at last the great beech trees on the opposite bank of the stream showed their new leaves and the garden began to fill with colour. The summer visitors returned, and one day one of them, a lady of mature years, came down the long flight of steps that led up to the road and knocked at our door. She told us that she had once lived in the house and would like to see it again, if we didn't mind. Of course we were pleased to show her around, and it emerged that her memories went back to the war years, when evacuees had been billeted there. She said the house had not changed in outside appearance, although owners before us had somewhat altered the internal layout. However, as she chatted with us, I thought her eye strayed occasionally to the kitchen window, as if she half expected to see something there; and once she blinked and looked away, as though something had startled her.

I suppose I should have asked her about the figure that had flickered for so long at the edge of my vision, but it seemed such an odd thing to ask a stranger in the clear light of a sunny morning that I hesitated, and the moment passed.

After our visitor had left a curious thing happened; the trick of the light (as I still described it to myself) seemed to repeat itself over and over as I went to and fro through the kitchen, although previously its appearances had been several days apart. I felt as though I was being reproached for my unwillingness to acknowledge it.

Then one day my denial (because that is what it had become) was challenged; my mother told me that she had from time to time seen (but from the living room window) the fleeting impression of a female figure passing along the terrace, which, like me, she had at first interpreted as my sister Alex. I had never spoken to her about what I had seen, and I had to think quickly before replying. In view of her concern over my father and her own nervous and imaginative nature, I decided still to say nothing, except to offer my theory about the glass.

A few days later however, looking alarmed, she said to me, 'Your father's seen her now!' Apparently he had suddenly got up from his chair in the living room and said to her 'Alex is here!' She had pointed out that Alex's car was not on the drive, but he had insisted, saying that Alex had just gone past the window. He had even gone out to look for her. I still said nothing about what I had seen, but tried to reassure her as best I could.

Sadly, my father died later that year. I remember that it was a beautiful October; sunny and mild, the clarity of the light bringing out the soft Autumn colours. On the evening of the funeral, as we were seeing off the last of our guests at the door, a wren flew down out of the darkness and landed on my shoulder; then it flew into the house, once around the living room and out again. That night as I looked up at the wicket gate that led to the road, high above the culvert, I saw a huge full moon looking down at me through the bars of the gate. There was a magic about the place, a sense of timelessness, of somewhere secret and set apart, that drew me to it; but I felt that spending long days alone there while I was at work was not fair to my mother, so we moved away.

The strain of my father's last illness had told on all of us. On the day of the move my mother became ill, and left early with my sister. It was a hot, still, day. When I was alone, clearing up after the removal men, the presence at the window once again became more insistent, repeating over and over that fleeting impression that had not changed since I first saw it. The atmosphere in the house felt oppressive. A bluebottle strayed in; its angry buzzing followed me from room to room. I realised I was becoming reluctant to approach the window, but I told myself not to be ridiculous. When I looked directly at it, there was nothing there. At last I was finished, and with a mingled sense of relief and regret I got into my car. As I set off up the drive for the last time a thrush darted almost under my wheels, uttering its alarm call and causing me to brake instinctively. The bird perched at the side of the drive and looked at me; I looked back at it. Then I drove away.

I still loved the house, despite the sad, and sometimes strange, things that had happened there, so some years later when I saw a gallery offering to have a watercolour painting done by a local artist 'from your favourite photograph', I took the opportunity.

When I called to collect the painting, the assistant said, 'The artist said to tell you he didn't know whether you wanted him to include the figure, but he put it in anyway.'

I knew what I would see, even before unwrapping the picture. There is the house, viewed from across the stream, on a brilliantly sunny day, with the garden full of colour; and there, on the terrace, she stands. The figure is only about two centimetres high; no details are visible, but it is clearly female; tall, judging by the door frame behind her; and, despite the stick that she appears to be holding, quite straight-backed. There was, of course, no figure in the photograph.

I never attempted to explain it. I never contacted the artist to discover whether the assistant had somehow misreported him. I felt that to do so would be a betrayal. If after trying to deny her I had inadvertently granted the mysterious presence the acknowledgement that she was seeking, then to try to take it back would be wrong - and might be unwise. Some things are best left alone. The house has been substantially altered by later owners, and the terrace, or that part of it, has been built over; but the picture still hangs on my wall, and in it the lady still stands looking at me over her garden, in the sunshine. Each time I pass it, I'm glad to see she's there.

One last thought occurs. I don't know what impelled me to write her story; I've never written anything before. The lady still watches me; but perhaps that's no longer enough.

Perhaps, as you read these words, she watches you.

Appropriation
Michael James Parker

MICHAEL JAMES PARKER is a struggling amateur author striving to become a struggling professional author. His work has appeared in Dark Chapter Press anthologies *Flashes of Darkness*, and their upcoming anthology *Edge of Darkness*. He was also winner of their January 2016 monthly flash fiction contest. He lives, works and writes in Middlesbrough.

'LOOK AT THESE!' she said, before she'd even closed the front door.
 'How can I look at something when you're not in the same room as me?'
 'These, Paul, aren't they brilliant?'
 Jess bounced into the lounge and stopped in the doorway, casting a critical glance around the room, taking in the empty coffee mug and its unused coaster and the empty crisp packets next to it and the discarded biscuit wrappers which had been rolled into little foil balls and, from the looks of things, chucked into an empty pizza box also on the table. She noted the console controller and the paused game and Paul's red-rimmed eyes. He hadn't even gotten dressed; he still wore the same stained jogging bottoms he'd had on when she left twelve hours earlier.
 'What are they?' Paul asked, leaning forward.
 In her hand, Jess held a pair of what looked to be sandals. The frustration of coming home to find him sitting there like a slob had taken some of the sheen from the shopper's euphoria she had been experiencing, but upon

being asked the question she perked back up again.

'They're hair sandals.'

Paul blinked at her. 'Hair?'

'Yeah. Hair.'

She held them out for him to touch, and he reached out with a finger and ran the tip down the side of one. He pulled the finger back and shook his head.

'No, I don't like that; it's weird. Are they real hair?'

'Yeah. The guy didn't have a clue what he had. He thought they were reproduction, but anyone with half a brain can see they're not.'

Paul looked at them. They were misshapen, with sunken toes and dented heels which looked to have been stamped almost flat. The leather soles were scuffed and almost worn right through in one or two places. In fact, the left one had an actual hole in it roughly the size of a five-pence piece. Someone had actually *worn* the things. 'Why did you buy them?'

Jess stared at him. 'Why wouldn't I? Have you ever seen anything like them? They're totally unique; they'll get so many hits on Instagram. Carol's already asked me to bring them to work on Monday so we can put them up on display. She wants me to wear them for a shoot, too. People will come to see these, I know it.'

Paul shook his head and picked up the controller.

'Aren't you even a little bit curious about them?'

He looked again. They were interesting, to be fair, definitely unusual, and she was right, they were just what the curio shop was missing. Ever since she'd bought a stake in it, she'd tried to drum up business, tried to convert online traffic into physical visitors. They may well get a few more bodies through the door.

Standing, he went to the TV and switched it, and his game, off.

'So,' he said, putting the crisp packets into the empty pizza box and carrying it and his coffee cup into the kitchen, raising his voice as he went, 'tell me about them, then.'

Jess smiled, feeling guilty for almost kicking off about the state of the living room, and the stained checked shirt and grotty jogging bottoms he still wore, and the fact that he'd clearly not moved from the sofa save to collect a pizza and make coffee; yet she was pleased with herself for having the discipline *not* to kick off. She was trying, she thought, and so was he. She waited until he was back in the sitting room.

'I looked them up online before I bought them. Pretended I was checking my banking app, didn't want to give away how eager I was. They were traditional in Asia. China, mainly, and they were normally made by widows for their husbands to be buried in. The widows, they'd cut off all their own hair. . .'

'Hang on,' Paul said. 'Their hair?'

'Yeah, they're hair sandals. What did you think I meant?'

'I thought you meant horsehair or something.'

'No, they're human. At least, they were, like, traditionally. And I think these might be a traditional pair. The widow would put them on her husband's feet. They were supposed to help them find each other in the afterlife.'

'Ah, I don't know about having them in here. Will you not take them to the shop?'

'Paul, I've been driving for ages. I don't want to drive to the shop as well, not this late. I'll take them tomorrow.'

'First thing, mind,' he said, staring at the sandals hanging limply from Jess's right hand. He shuddered.

'It's not *that* bad! Mr. Melodrama. So what did you do today while I was out?'

'Just a little bit of gaming. What makes you think those things are traditional?'

Jess set the sandals on her palms and studied them. They sagged inward and bowed outward and looked just generally dishevelled enough to be old. 'I think because they're so crudely made. You can tell a machine hasn't been anywhere near these. I mean, look: this one is clearly bigger than the other,' she waggled her right hand, then set the sandals down on her lap, flipping them over as she did so. 'And then, there's the stitching. Look at those irregular stitches – they've been done by hand.'

Paul saw again the age-worn soles, burnished almost entirely smooth over the years. Something about those crinkled soles made his skin crawl.

He thought of his dad's irrational fear of buttons, instilled after having been jokingly threatened with decapitation and having a button sewn on in his head's stead for bad behaviour, and wondered if something along the same lines had happened with shoes in his own formative years, hit with a slipper for being naughty or something, maybe. Those kinds of things stuck, he knew, and caused weird phobias later in life.

When she'd finished, she set them on the floor and slid her feet out of her own shoes.

'You're not,' Paul said.

'What are you so scared of?'

He couldn't rightly say; his creeping sense of fear was impossible to explain. 'I'd just rather you didn't.'

'Well, I'm going to be wearing them at some point anyway, so why not here?'

She slipped one foot into the sandal, and then the other, feeling the gentle caress of the hairs which had broken and come away from the main structure of the shoe, and the soft suppleness of the soles hug her feet like a second skin. Wiggling her toes, she stood up and walked to the full-length mirror in the hallway and back again. The soles slid a little on the wooden flooring, but she otherwise padded silently in them.

'They feel fantastic on!' she said.

'Alright, you've made your point. Take them off, now, please, darling; they're giving me the creeps.'

Jess gave an exaggerated sigh and sat on the arm of the sofa, crossing her right leg over her left. She pulled at the heel. She frowned. Pulled at the heel again. Then again, this time with both hands. Her forearms bulged with effort.

'They won't come off.'

'Shut up.'

Jess tried again, hooking her fingers inside and pulling hard enough for her bicep to twitch against the fabric of her t-shirt.

'Pack it in, Jess.'

She stood up. 'Paul, this isn't me. Help!' she said, whipping her head frantically and walking back towards the hall.

She disappeared behind the door.

'Pau–'

'Jess?'

Paul sat on the edge of his seat.

'Jess?' he said a third time, standing up.

Nothing.

'Stop pissing around, Jess, I mean it.'

Still nothing.

'Jess, you're not . . .'

'Paul, come quickly!' she cried.

He sprang over the arm of the sofa and into the open doorway, where he found Jess in front of the mirror in her long blue trenchcoat.

'Look at how well they go with this coat,' she said, laughing. 'Jesus, your face – you look like you're about to cry. Fancy a pair of sandals getting you so worked up.' She took one last glance in the mirror, posing with one heel lifted, then the other, and then she carefully took the sandals off.

'That wasn't funny.'

'It was. What do you want to do?'

In the end, they watched TV, which began as it always did, with Jess getting up to use the toilet a few times and then falling asleep. Paul was a few episodes into *iZombie* (a show Jess believed to be stupid and pointless, and thus a show he watched mainly alone, or after she'd fallen asleep) when he noticed a shadowy blur at the edge of their TV screen. He looked around the room for the cause of it, thinking perhaps the lampshade had been knocked askew or something, but he couldn't see any obvious culprit. Glancing back at the TV, he saw the blurred section had darkened.

'Must be screen burn,' he said to himself, remembering having paused the game for a while. It irked him, though; the TV was only a few months old. He'd have to dig the receipt out of the drawers tomorrow morning. If it hadn't been victim to one of Jess's regular purges, that was.

He peeked at her, her head resting on a pillow against his hip, hands clutching the throw blanket around her shoulders. Placing a hand on her back, he shook her gently awake.

'Hmm?'

'It's getting late, darling. Let's go to bed.'

'Okay,' she said, rubbing her eyes and shrugging the throw from her. She swung her legs down from the sofa.

Paul did a double-take.

'I asked you not to wear them, Jess, I think they're weird.'

'Wear what?'

Paul pointed at her feet. The sandals covered them like furry socks.

Jess blinked the fug of sleep away. She'd slipped them on when she went to the toilet, that much she recalled, and though she thought she'd taken them off, she must have forgotten. 'Sorry,' she said, 'I was messing with them on my way to the toilet.'

'Well, can you please leave them down here?'

She nodded as she slid her feet out of them again and set them neatly by the side of the sofa. She left the room, Paul following behind. He waited until she knocked on the passage light before flicking off the lamp and closing the door behind him.

The passage floor was cold and Jess felt a pang of longing for the sandals, warm and comfortable despite their dilapidated appearance. The soles of her feet prickled under the rub of the stair carpet.

They took turns to use the toilet and brush their teeth, and while Jess removed her make-up Paul went into the bedroom to warm the bed up.

He didn't remember falling asleep (who ever does?), but he woke with a start when he heard the *click* of the bathroom door. The clock showed two a.m. Jess, toilet like clockwork, he thought, and rolled over. The bed was empty, covers on Jess's side rumpled and pulled back. He heard her footsteps and a second later she appeared in the doorway, hair teased and tangled by sleep's invisible fingers. She clambered back into bed and snuggled under the covers. He planted a kiss on her back and turned away, drifting off immediately.

Another *click* woke him, followed by slow, heavy footsteps. He scrunched his eyes at the clock until the green blur of the LCD clock face showed three sixteen a.m. With one eye on the door, he waited for Jess to reappear in the doorway and made a mental note to have a talk about the frequency of her nightly toilet trips when they got up in the morning.

He rolled over, flipped his pillow to the cool side, and froze.

Jess was in the bed next to him. He could see her huddled under the covers. The pale form of her hand extended out from beneath the blanket.

Instant icy prickles needled every square inch of his skin. Logic centres in his brain tried to explain the sounds to him. Perhaps she'd made them and gotten back into bed before he'd fully woken, or maybe the sounds were just memories of a dream he'd been having. Or perhaps someone was in the house. A burglar. A smackhead trying to steal the telly. The footsteps grew closer. Each thudding step sent his heart rate soaring, drumming so loudly he could hear it.

Trembling, he reached over and shook Jess awake.

The footsteps stopped in the doorway.

'What are you doing?' she asked.

Paul couldn't remember the last time he screamed such a full-throated scream. If he'd had time to think about it, he'd probably say he'd never screamed in such a way in all of his adult life. He *shrieked*. Felt his vocal chords strain under the pressure. He simultaneously turned to the doorway, saw Jess standing there, her mouth agape, and pushed himself away from the bed, his feet brushing against something solid inside of something soft and tickly under the duvet.

Jess's scream joined his in a horrified duet.

He was sprawled on the floor when the bedsprings creaked and a pale form rose from the gloom. The light switch clicked and the room filled with a sickly yellow glow, illuminating a figure crouched on the bed. The light gleamed off its bald, cadaver-pale head, highlighting nicks and cuts and slivers of shiny white skull. Flaps of skin which had once been breasts hung limply from its chest, the nipples dark splotches on skin as thin and veined as batwings. Its stomach had two large, ovoid swathes of skin missing, revealing ancient, slimy grey musculature beneath like rancid meat.

Head swivelling on its impossibly thin neck, the thing, this ancient crone, shifted its Asiatic eyes from Paul, to Jess, to Paul, extending a tremulous finger at him as he lay vulnerable on the bedroom floor.

The thing glared at the bulb. It extinguished in a second, plunging the room into darkness once more. The bedroom door slammed shut. Jess wailed and slid down it. A hot wetness spread across Paul's lap. In the darkness, Paul heard the whisper-soft shuffle of feet. Fetid breath assailed his nostrils and moistened his cheek. He screamed again.

It took him, curling its bony fingers around his throat in a pincer grip. The room became a kiln, ripe with the smell of burnt carpet fibre and sizzling pork and singed hair, and then Paul's scream ceased, and Jess saw the shadow where he'd been lying vanish.

The crone unfolded from its crouched position, standing taller than Jess could believe, and stalked towards her.

The Lengthsman
Charles Wilkinson

Charles Wilkinson's publications include *The Snowman and Other Poems* (IRON Press, 1987), *The Pain Tree* and Other Stories (London Magazine Editions, 2000) and *Ag & Au*, (Flarestack Poets, 2013). His collection of strange tales and weird fiction, *A Twist in the Eye*, is now out from Egaeus Press. He lives in Powys, Wales, where he is heavily outnumbered by members of the ovine community.

'THE DEAD WALK right through that gate there. You won't see them proper, like. Just shapes. And you'll hear their footsteps, ever so soft on the grass; then louder on the gravel. But you can't miss the candle – right at the head of the procession, moving at about the height of a man's chest. Though there's no hand holding it.'
Rhodri was leaning forward on a tombstone, his arms folded like a farmer's. He had a pale oval face and mousy hair with a shine more grey than brown, almost as if made out of metal.
 'Have you seen them?' asked Timothy, who was just that much younger.
 Rhodri gazed round the graveyard. He was related to everyone in it. For a moment, Timothy thought his friend looked like one of the duty masters at boarding school, making sure all the boys were tucked up for the night before he flicked the switch.
 'I wonder how many types of grass there are here,' said Rhodri, moving away from the tombstone.

Timothy got to his feet and followed him towards the church. There was a slight breeze off the grey-blue mountains to the west, where Rhodri's ancestors had mastered the longbow. Cloud-shadow pencilled over a wheat field in the valley below, turning gold to grey. Rhodri claimed the creeper on the rectory's pale orange brick wall turned an unfamiliar shade of red identical to dragon's blood.

'Really rotten, it is,' said Rhodri. 'You not going back to school for two weeks after we've started.'

'It's because we have to work on Saturdays.'

Rhodri hopped off the path and used Timothy's ruler to slash at the long grass by the tombstones, the ones where the inscriptions had vanished beneath verdure. But even after this attack nothing legible emerged. The dark stone had started to flake; thin white worms of words were blurred by lichen.

Every year, in the last days of summer and the first few weeks of autumn, Timothy's parents rented the low cottage on the far side of the churchyard. The owner was an old friend and their son's godmother. The leaves were falling earlier this year, which made the whole business of going back to boarding school in a week and a half worse. He thought of the great white Georgian barn of a building, its playing fields and woods, the colours already reduced for winter; the sheaves of muddied gold shovelled into wheelbarrows. He had foreknowledge of part of what was to come. After one poor examination result, extra work had been set for the holidays; the mornings were devoted to Maths.

'May I have my ruler?'

Rhodri executed three more scything strokes before tossing it back. Several inches on both sides were stained green.

Before he went to bed Timothy remembered how when he was very young he asked for a night light. That night he dreamt he had woken up to find his squat candle had been exchanged for a tall wax one, on which the hours were written in Roman numerals.

'Who changed it?' he cried, although he was not aware of anyone nearby.

'The lengthsman,' said a voice, 'I do all the measuring here.'

Timothy stood by the basin and watched his father shave: the brush dipped in water so the badger's hair, which had been soft to touch, was sharpened to a dark wet point; then it was rubbed on a shaving stick until the lather was thick and creamy. The shaving mirror was on a walnut cabinet next to an enamel basin. Timothy passed his forefinger over his jaw, imitating the razor's action. It was hard to imagine the day when his skin would lose its rubbery smoothness and become rough and scratchy. As the foam was shaved away, Timothy saw how his father's flesh was pinker than before; a few tiny specks of blood on the Adam's apple.

'Do you enjoy shaving, Daddy?'

He laughed. 'Not particularly. It's just something you have to do unless you want to grow a beard.'

'How often?'

'Every morning.'

'Will I have to shave?' he asked, even though he knew the answer.

'Of course. Although not every day to start with.'

The white lather in the basin was flecked with fine black hairs. His father pulled out the plug; the water drained away, slowly at first; then with a final swirl and gurgle.

'What will we do in Maths?' Timothy was hoping for triangles and circles. Anything but incomprehensible algebra.

His father opened the window and peered out. A fine day with a china blue sky: summer's last gesture in the face of falling leaves.

'We'll give Maths a miss. You've not long left before you go back. Go down to the castle, if you want. Your mother and I have people coming for coffee this morning. Boring people.'

'Which boring people?'

'Well not boring people. That's a little unfair. People from the church. I don't think you'd find them interesting.'

'Rhodri says that the rector used to play cards with the Devil, but he lost fifty per cent of the games he played and that's why half of his body is buried in the churchyard and the rest under the oak tree outside the church gates.'

His father wiped his razor and sighed. 'If you have to play with Rhodri at least try not to listen to anything he says.'

'How long is it before I have to go back?' he said. 'How many days?'

'Next week. Tuesday evenings for full boarders.'

The rugby term. And this time it wouldn't be just 'touch' for the first half of the season. He recalled the proper games he'd taken part in: the smell of mud and boys' wet shirts – his neck wrenched in the scrum as it wheeled; the boots flying at the break down; the pointy elbows in the rucks and mauls; the sharp hard tackle that took him off his feet so the field rose up, slamming a door of earth into his face and chest; and how, as he got up groggily, silver stars circled about his head.

Timothy decided to go down to the river. It was a Saturday. If he went to the church or the castle first, he was certain to run into Rhodri and the others. There was a quiet spot where he could watch the river's sluggish flow, the seams of sunlight shifting on its green surface. He would have company soon enough: the boys brushing their teeth in basins beside him; the queues moving into assembly and filing into classrooms with sash windows that stretched up to the ceiling; the roar of the changing-rooms – the heads accidentally knocked together during the search for missing rugby boots; the steam and pink bodies next to you under the hiss of the showers; the snores in the dormitory.

His godmother had fishing rights on a stretch of the river. There was a wooden lodge with a picket fence around it and an outside lavatory, the haunt of spiders, daddy-long-legs and beetles.

Just as he was about to fetch the key from its hiding place, he saw the door to the lodge was ajar. He opened the gate, went up the path and peered in: a line of waders and wellington boots as well as rods and waxed jackets on hooks. The room smelled of dust. Afterwards he was unable to decide what had made him turn round. Perhaps it was an almost imperceptible adjustment to the quality of the light. The man was standing halfway along the path with his back to the sun. He was the tallest and thinnest person Timothy had ever seen. Although he was wearing brown trousers and a tweed jacket the colour of grey moss, he was not dressed for a day's fishing. His narrow face was firewood dry, yet creased and stained like old leather. He seemed cornered by shadows.

'What are you doing here?' asked Timothy.

'I look after the things at the edge. Do a bit of tidying up, cutting down. But don't worry; you're not on the verge today.'

The man's mouth was no deeper than a scratch on slate, but as the words were spoken there was no movement on his face, not the slightest motion in the line that passed for lips. The voice was one that Timothy recognised. But which direction did it come from? It might even have been inside his head. He went straight back into the lodge and shut the door. He waited for a knock or a face ancient as oak peering through the window. Nothing happened.

When at last he was ready, he opened the door to the gleam on the river and the light on russet leaf. A perfect noon. Except for a long shadow lying across the path that could not be accounted for by the presence of any nearby object or the angle of the sun.

The smack hard on the shoulder blades and his right leg taken from under him; then Timothy was tumbling into the grassy dry moat, the startled sheep racing under the wooden bridge and round the curtain wall. As he rolled down, snapshots of masonry, turf, battlements spun around him, repeating in quick succession. From above came the sound of familiar laughter. Fortunately the grass at the bottom was lush and springy. He picked himself up. Meurig Morgan, his blaze of red hair more unruly than ever, was dancing and dodging along the top of the moat, ready to push Timothy back again, no matter which route up he selected.

'*Sais*,' shouted Meurig, '*sais*!' He stooped to pick something up; then a clod of earth accompanied by pebbles passed over Timothy's head.

'Careful!' yelled Timothy. He was halfway up the incline and wondering whether it might be a better idea to run back and then sprint round to the other side of the castle.

Meurig was bare-footed, which explained how he had managed to creep up so silently. At least there was no sign of his four brothers. The boy's normally white skin was flushed with excitement and exertion. He knelt down to gather further ammunition.

'All right, that's enough for now.' Rhodri must have emerged from the narrow gateway at the far end of the bridge. That part of the castle was surprisingly intact. If you looked up, you could see the murder holes from which boiling oil had been poured.

Meurig, who had been on the point of letting loose another volley, hesitated. Then a handful of sticks and small stones fell to the earth. It was strange how the other village boys always accepted Rhodri's decisions without argument even though he lacked their wiry strength. Perhaps it was to do with the power of his stories.

Seeing Rhodri walk to the other side of the bridge, Meurig turned in the direction of the village.

'What was that he said?'

'*Sais*. It's our name for you lot. A term of abuse, I'd call it.'

As Timothy clambered up the bank, Rhodri advanced a few yards down, held out an arm and hauled him to the top.

'Thanks. That Meurig's the worst of the Morgans. He could have put my eye out.'

'Oh ignore him,' said Rhodri good humouredly. 'In his blood, it is. Perfectly natural for a Morgan to want to drive out an invader. Anyway what are you doing around here admiring your castle? I thought it was Maths again for you.'

'I was given the morning off. And it's not my castle. It's just an old ruin.'

'Your lot built it and your lot knocked it down. Don't you know that?'

'I think we're doing castles next term.'

'Centuries of oppression, my da says!'

Still breathing heavily, Timothy put his hands on his hips. 'I've had rather an odd time. I meet a tall man down by the river. '

'What? Longshanks come back to bother us again?'

'Who's he?'

'Oh never mind. What was so strange about him then?'

'I can't explain. He was…well, I don't think his name is Longshanks, but he might be a lengthsman. Do you know what a lengthsman does?'

'You have to be careful down by rivers. Watch how you cross.'

'Why?'

'Easy to get dragged down. Then even if you're not dead, you could find yourself in another world.'

Timothy was sitting in the back of the Daimler trying not to feel sick in the leather and petrol smell. His grey flannel jacket and shorts felt heavy; the hot ring of his white collar, which his stripy tie had fixed too close to his neck, was uncomfortable. New leather shoes chafed the back of his heels. He had been told he looked very smart.

'I'm sorry we've got to drop you off early,' said his father, eyes firmly fixed on the road ahead. 'But there will be a few others boys there. We phoned the school to check.'

The landscape was flatter and the light had lost the watery mystery of the Marches.

They passed through the edge of a town, the road lined by pollarded trees and matter-of-fact houses.

'Daddy.'

'Yes.'

'You know Rhodri's stories?'

'Unfortunately.'

'How many of them do you think are true?'

'Absolutely none.'

'Rhodri's grandfather was a collector of folk tales,' put in Timothy's mother, although she seldom spoke when he was being driven back to school. 'He was the rector in the village, wasn't he dear?' she said, turning to her husband.

'I believe he was.'

The fields were wider now with neatly clipped hedges.

'Rhodri says the English knocked down the castle.'

'Well, he is right about that. A rare example of accuracy on Rhodri's behalf. Cromwell's men were responsible.'

Timothy started to recognise the names of villages, a distinctive church spire, a pub with a wagon wheel outside.

'Daddy what's a lengthsman?'

There was silence as his father stopped at a cross road.

'A lengthsman. Where did you come across that word?'

'I don't know. It keeps coming into my head.'

'Well, there's nothing sinister about it. As far as I can remember, a lengthsman is someone employed to keep a parish tidy. Trim the verges. Look it up in the dictionary when you get back to school. Switch the radio on, dear,' he added, glancing at his wife.

It was not yet dark when they reached the long drive that led up to the school. As they passed through stone gates surmounted by two grey pineapples, Timothy shifted in his seat. The backs of his bare thighs felt sticky as they peeled away from the leather. As yet there were no lights on in the cold white barracks of a house at the top of the hill. The posts were up on the junior colts pitch where he'd have to play. Someone in his form had told him about a boy who died in a rugby match at another school when the scrum collapsed. He wondered if that was a story, just like one of Rhodri's.

They were coming up to the Ist XV's big field when Timothy saw him. Too tall to be remotely in proportion with his surroundings, the lengthsman was marking out the touchline closest to the drive. There was a tape measure and pegs hammered into the ground. Although the man had his back to him, Timothy recognised him at once. As he wheeled the marker, he left a long white line behind him.

'We'll drop your trunk off, but I hope you won't mind if we don't come in, old boy. Must make headway while it's still light. You can manage your tuck box, can't you?'

As they drew level with the lengthsman, the car slowed down for a speed bump. The long thin head, now more totem than flesh, turned towards Timothy. The eyes were still there, but the mouth was hidden in the grain.

'Are you all right there in the back?' asked his father.

Timothy tried to speak, but the words wouldn't come. If he looked round, would he see the lengthsman abandon his task to come lolloping after them like something out of legend? He raised both hands to his face. His skin had lost its rubbery resilience; its texture was soft, not a surface that would ever be shaved.

The Light Left
Jane Ayrie

JANE AYRIE writes short and long fiction ranging from the lightly humorous to the darkly macabre. She lives in York and her varied but never rich career includes stints as an encyclopaedia sales person, life model, counsellor and assorted roles in social services. She is a regular contributor to the website ABCtales.com and is currently writing a science fiction novel.

'THAT BLOODY LIGHT's gone again,' said Bo.

Ally looked up from her muesli. 'The one on the landing?'

Bo looked irritated. 'I put a new bulb in yesterday. Perhaps it's the socket thing.'

'Could be.' Ally looked at her watch. 'Or could be a dud bulb. Try another one, see how it goes. I better get off.'

Bo looked at Ally's bowl and mug. 'Put them in the dishwasher before you go.'

Ally gave what she hoped was a loving, non-irritated smile. 'Yes ma'am.'

'We made a deal,' Bo said.

Ally stood up and kissed her. 'I know. Working at home doesn't make you a housewife.' She brushed back a stray lock of Bo's curly brown hair and kissed her again. 'Just *my* wife. Lucky, lucky me.'

'Go to work,' said Bo, a smile snagging the corner of her mouth. 'Pick up some of those cat treat things, will you, on your way home? I forgot to get some yesterday.'

Ally stepped out of the front door to a shock of winter air and the beginnings of winter sunshine. The roofs of the houses at the other end of the street, where the sun had not yet reached, still glistened with frost, and tiny diamond sparkles littered parts of the pavement. It was a light, bright day. Ally set off towards the main road at a brisk pace.

She revelled in the novelty of being able to walk to work. Just one of the reasons she had been so taken with the little terraced house, and grateful that they could afford it due to the reduction for a quick sale. Even after just a week it felt like theirs. Hers and Bo's. Their married home.

It was her first day back at work, and there were emails to trawl through and minutes of meetings to skim and voicemails from clients to decipher. She saw the notification of a voicemail from Bo on her own phone while showing the honeymoon photos round, but there was no time to listen to the message until she broke for coffee at eleven. By which time there were three voicemails.

'Hi babes, I tried a new bulb in that light but it won't work. And the one in our bedroom is flickering now. I think it might be the wiring. Isn't Anne's husband an electrician? I wondered if you could have a word. Might be cheaper than just picking someone at random. See you later. Love you.'

'Ally, there's definitely something wrong with the wiring. All the lights are off. And the other thing, I don't know if it's connected, my phone won't work. I'm having to call from the landline. Well, actually, I don't know if it's working. The screen won't light up, so I can't get into it. Anyway. If you could have a word with Anne. Love you.'

'Ally, it's really weird. Not one of the lights will work. The light on the kettle. The light in the fridge. The things work, I mean, the kettle boils and the fridge is cold. There's just...no light. And the cat won't come in. Can you ring me, Ally? Please. Love you.'

Ally phoned. 'Hi, sweetie.'

'Al, I don't know what's going on.'

'OK, calm down, just tell me what's happened. Calm down, Bo.'

Bo said, 'You think I'm making it up, don't you?'

Ally closed her eyes. 'No, sweetie, no, of course not. Of course I don't think that. I think it's a bit weird, you said that yourself. Obviously, there's something wrong with the wiring, and maybe there's some sort of …I don't know, static or something, and it's affecting the other electrical stuff.'

'Maybe that's why the cat won't come in,' said Bo. 'Maybe he can sense the…the static. Have you spoken to Anne?'

'She's not in, sweetie. She doesn't work Mondays and Tuesdays.'

'Ally, we have to do something.'

'I'll ask around. See if someone can recommend an electrician. Don't worry, sweets, we'll get it sorted. Is the heating still working?'

'Yes. But the display light thing isn't on. Ally, my laptop won't work. I can hear the motor thing and I put a CD in and it played, but the screen's dead. I've got work due on Thursday.'

'It'll be all right. I'll sort it.'

'I wish the cat would come in. Ally, can you get home early?'

Ally rubbed her forehead. 'Sweetie, I can't. I've just got so much to catch up on.'

'I don't know what's going on. Ally, please try and come home.'

Ally got a recommendation for an electrician, called him at lunchtime and left a voicemail, saying it was urgent.

She phoned Bo on the landline. 'Hi, sweetie.'

'Can you come home?'

'No, darling, I really can't. Listen, I've got the name of an electrician, and I've phoned and left a message. I've said it's urgent and I've given him the landline number.'

'Why? You said you were going to sort it.'

After a moment Ally said, 'He'll need to organise with you when he can come round. Otherwise it means he has to ring me and I have to ring you and then I have to ring him back. I thought it would be quicker.'

Bo said, 'The cat still won't come in.'

'Don't worry about the cat. Still getting used to the new house, I expect. Probably hasn't forgiven us for putting him in the cattery while we were away.'

'It'll be dark soon,' said Bo.

Ally looked out of the window. The lemon winter sun beamed from a cloudless sky. 'Not for a few hours yet.'

Bo said, 'It'll be all right if you're here. I won't mind the dark if you're with me. Can't you come home, Ally?'

'Sweetie, I can't. Don't worry. I expect the electrician will ring soon. Love you.'

Ally sat looking at the phone. Of course I should go home, she thought. She's my wife. I love her. She needs me.

But it's only the bloody wiring. I've rung the electrician. I've made all the arrangements. I've sorted everything out. As usual.

She looked out at the light, bright day. She'd known there would be days like this, when Bo couldn't cope with simple things, like answering the phone or sorting out the cat or getting the washing out of the machine. But normally there was some sort of warning, time to get ready, to contact the doctor if necessary. Not just a bolt out of the blue of a brilliant winter sky, on the first day Bo was alone in the house.

For better or for worse. In sickness and in health.

It took some organising, and her manager wasn't pleased, but an hour and a half later Ally was walking briskly back along the main road, her phone to her ear. 'Bo, I've been trying to ring you. Please pick up, sweetie. Has the electrician called? I'm on my way home, I'll be about fifteen minutes. Love you. Lots.'

There had been no call from Bo when she turned into their street. The pavement was no longer sparkling and the frost had vanished from all the rooftops. The elderly lady from two doors down was just coming out as Ally approached.

'Hello dear, settling in all right? I saw your...*other half* this morning, calling the cat in.'

Ally smiled. Mrs Barrett seemed like a nice lady, trying to adjust to a changing world. 'Yes, thank you. I think we've settled in better than the cat. Except – do you know if the Lindleys ever had any problem with the wiring?'

Mrs Barrett stopped. 'The wiring, dear?'

'Yes. The lights are playing up. I don't suppose it's anything major. The survey didn't show up any problem. I just wondered if the Lindleys ever said anything.'

'No,' said Mrs Barrett. She started to edge past Ally. 'I have to go, dear, I'll miss my bus. Give my regards to your… other half.' She hesitated. 'Is she all right, dear?'

'How do you mean?'

'Your…other half. Does she have any problems, dear? You know.' Mrs Barrett leaned closer. 'Personal difficulties?'

'What?'

'Only, I might be able to help, dear, if you can't get it fixed. I have a friend, who might be able to help. Must go, dear. My bus…' She almost pushed Ally aside. 'Good luck, dear.'

'Thank you,' said Ally, to the old lady's retreating back.

'Bo?' she called, as she opened the front door. 'It's me, sweetie. I'm here.' She closed the door behind her.

The house felt dark.

Ally flicked the light switch. Nothing happened. She moved along the hall into the kitchen.

'Bo?'

She looked out of the kitchen window. The mellowing afternoon sun would soon start to fade. The window was large, and the back door was glass, but the kitchen felt dark.

Ally opened the fridge. It was cold, but there was no light. She flicked the switch on the kettle and within seconds it started to heat, but the indicator light stayed dark.

Bo's phone was on the worktop. Ally picked it up and swiped the screen. It stayed black. She took her own phone from her bag and repeated the process, with the same result. She stepped back into the hall.

'Bo?'

There was a sound from upstairs, light footsteps on the landing, a slight creak as their bedroom door opened.

'Sweetie? Has the electrician called?'

The hall was silent.

Ally started walking up the stairs, her phone in her hand. At the top was the door to the bathroom, and then the galleried landing doubled back, with the spare bedroom first, and then their bedroom at the front of the house. As she turned on to the landing, she saw that their bedroom door was slightly ajar. It closed, softly, as she approached.

Ally stopped. The landing was almost completely dark. 'Bo?'

There was a soft click as the door opened slightly.

'Bo?'

Ally pushed the door fully open. Ahead was the window; the curtains were drawn and she thought, they're not lined and it's still sunny out there. Why is it so dark?

She stepped forward and looked round the door, towards the bed.

Bo's back was pressed against the wooden headboard, her knees hunched up to her chin, arms wrapped round her legs, fingers interlocked in front of her calves. She was looking toward the opposite corner, the one just beside the window.

'Sweetie?' Ally half ran to the bed, concern sweeping everything else from her mind. 'Sweetie, are you OK?' She sat down and placed her own hands over Bo's. 'Sweetie?'

'We'll be all right,' Bo whispered, her eyes fixed on the corner by the window. 'It'll be dark soon.'

Ally tried to unlock Bo's fingers. 'Come on baby, let's go downstairs. Please. Let's go down. I'll make you a cup of tea.'

'We're safe up here. It's darker up here.'

Tears rolled down Ally's cheeks. 'Oh sweetie...'

'We're safe in the dark,' said Bo.

Ally felt the coldness start at the nape of her neck, spreading up through her skull and down along her spine. She thought about how the bedroom door had closed when she was on the landing, and opened again, and about how she had not heard any sound as Bo moved across the room and got on to the bed. Slowly, she moved her head.

The corner was empty.

Ally felt sick. She pulled at Bo's hands. 'Come on, darling. We have to go. We need to get out of here.'

Bo twisted away from her. 'But it's not dark out there.'

'Bo, please.'

Bo's head turned.

Ally looked into the eyes that were not Bo's. She pulled her fingers away from unrecognised flesh.

'We need the dark,' said the voice that was not Bo's.

Ally pushed herself away from the bed. The face turned away from her.

In the dark corner, a blur, a greyness, a soft shape she knew, and with her mind rather than her senses, she heard Bo's small, distant voice: Ally... *Ally...*

'Give her back!' she screamed at the figure on the bed.

'We're safe in the dark.'

'Give her back!'

'We're safe.'

'*She's safe with me!*' Bo's voice in her mind. Ally. *Ally...*

The figure on the bed shuddered and twisted, straining towards the soft shape in the corner. The voice that was not Bo's started to croon. 'Stay with me. Please. We'll be safe in the dark if you stay with me.'

'She's not yours!' screamed Ally. 'She's mine! Bo! *Bo...*'

And this time she heard it echoing around the room, Bo's voice screeching, pleading, demanding: 'Let me go! *Let me go*! Please, *please* let me go!'

The figure jerked as if hit, fell back on the bed, and lay still.

Wisps of light filtered through the curtains.

'Ally?'

Ally watched the crumpled figure. Half sitting, half lying, it looked at her.

'Ally?'

She looked into Bo's eyes. She moved slowly forward and put out her hand. She felt Bo's flesh. She sat on the bed and took Bo's hand. Bo started to cry.

'It's all right,' Ally said. She put Bo's hand down. 'It's all right.'

Bo flung her arms round Ally's neck. 'I could see you. I was calling to you. You couldn't hear me.'

'I heard you,' said Ally. 'I heard you.'

They looked towards the empty corner.

Ally disengaged Bo's arms. 'We need to leave.'

As she stood up, Ally saw her phone, lying on the bedroom carpet. She must have dropped it in the darkness. She picked it up and looked at the screen, bright with the photo of her and Bo on their wedding day.

'We have to leave before it's dark,' she said.

Bo looked back towards the corner. 'It's gone, Ally. I can feel it.' She smiled. 'There's nothing to be afraid of now. Not now you're with me.'

'We have to leave,' said Ally. She looked at Bo's face, and a wave of nausea swept over her.

'But where will we go?'

'A hotel. For tonight.'

'What about the cat? And I've got a deadline for Thursday.'

Ally turned away. 'Then you stay.'

'You can't leave me,' said Bo.

Ally stood by the door. 'I'll ask Mrs Barrett to feed the cat. It's the least she can do.' She looked back at Bo. 'Are you coming?'

When they had put some essentials into a couple of holdalls, Ally rang a hotel and a taxi, disregarding a voicemail from the electrician.

It was nearly dark. Ally went through the house, putting on the lights.

'We can't just leave all the lights on, Ally.'

'Mrs Barrett can turn them off.'

When the taxi arrived they put the bags in the boot and Ally said, 'You get in. I'll take the keys to Mrs Barrett. I won't be a minute.'

Mrs Barrett's sitting room windows were bright, and when she opened the door light from the hall tumbled out on to the pavement.

'Hello dear!'

Ally said, 'What happened to the Lindleys?'

Mrs Barrett's fingers fluttered to her lips and she looked towards the taxi.

'Who is it?' Ally asked.

Mrs Barrett kept looking at the taxi. 'We didn't think it would be a problem, not for anyone else. We thought it was just poor Mrs Lindley.'

'Who is it?'

Mrs Barrett's eyes were sad. 'Mrs Carr, dear. That's who it is. Lived here, oh, forty years ago now. She was a bit touched, poor love. She thought everyone was looking at her all the time, and eventually she would only go out in the dark. Her husband did his best, but in the end he couldn't cope and he left her.'

'What happened to her?'

'She went to the hospital. She was there for years. Then they put her somewhere else, you know, when they closed all the big mental places down. That's where she died. I think it was her heart.'

'Then why is she here?'

Mrs Barrett looked thoughtful. 'I think this was where she was happy, dear, at first, with her husband. I think she came back to find him.' She shook her head. 'Such a shame. The Lindleys were all right until Mrs Carr passed away. Mrs Lindley, she'd not long lost a baby, see, and she was a bit fragile. That's why I asked about your...other half, if she was fragile. My friend's a medium, and we tried to help dear, we really did, but in the end they had to go, and they couldn't say anything because they needed to sell the house.' Her eyes finally flickered towards Ally. 'You understand, dear. It'll be the same for you now, I suppose. You'll want to move on. Quickly.'

'Here are the keys. Please will you feed the cat.' It was not a request. 'Until we get something sorted out.'

'Yes, dear. Of course.' Mrs Barrett looked towards the taxi again. 'Don't worry, dear, you'll put it behind you. Get back to normal.'

'Did the Lindleys?'

'I don't know, dear. They don't keep in touch.'

As the taxi turned out of the street Bo leant her head on Ally's shoulder. Instinctively, Ally dropped her chin to rest on the soft brown curls.

Bo put her hand in Ally's. 'We'll be all right,' she whispered. 'I can cope with anything, as long as you're with me. You won't leave me, Ally, will you?' She gripped Ally's fingers. 'You musn't leave me. You musn't.'

Ally raised her chin from Bo's head and looked out of the window, into the darkening night.

Ghosted
Matt Wesolowski

MATT WESOLOWSKI is an author from Newcastle upon Tyne. He is an English tutor for children in care and leads Cuckoo Young Writers creative writing workshops. Wesolowski started his writing career in horror and his short horror fiction has been published in numerous magazines and anthologies. Wesolowski was a winner of the Pitch Perfect competition at Bloody Scotland Crime Writing Festival 2015 and his debut crime novel *Six Stories* will be available through Orenda Books 2017.

Ghosting – *the act of suddenly ceasing all communication with someone the subject is dating, but no longer wishes to date. This is done in hopes that the ghostee will just 'get the hint' and leave the subject alone, as opposed to the subject simply telling them he/she is no longer interested.*
– *UrbanDictionary.com*

'When you moving her in then?'

Colm's nose is sweaty and I can see a bit of saag paneer clinging to his beard. Bollywood blares in the background. Forks and knives chitter against china. Benny bangs his fist on the table and snorts. A few heads turn our way.

'Steady on fellas.' I say.

I'm smiling a little.

We suckle on our pints for a bit; Colm and Benny's grins mould to the rim of their glasses as they look at me. I pick at the last few poppadoms; still grinning. Lime pickle throbs on the roof of my mouth.

They've not met her yet.

'Remember in primary,' Colm suppresses a burp with the back of his hand and points at me, 'when Jake called Miss McKay 'mum'?'

My phone buzzes, saving me.

'That'll be her now.'

The lads cheer. I grin, swollen with spice and pride.

Of course it's her.

Hope you're telling them nice stuff about me ;) xxx

I want to tell Colm and Benny about how even the thought of her sends an extra pulse into my arteries; how the touch of her, the taste of her lingers long after she's gone.

They'd get it. They'd understand.

I fill my mouth with jalfrezi instead.

I finish off the ant-powder today; it's sunny and I'm out the back door and into the alley around the side of the house. I pour it through the grate, the window to their lair. I clog their wings, speckle their abdomens as they crawl over each other, a squirming mass of languid legs and antennae.

I take a photo, hold my phone as close to the grate as I dare, ready to run if one flies out and lands on me. The last of the stuff will go inside, the corners, the cracks where the little horrors get in.

'You do the Shake and Vac,' I sing.

Horrible flying fuckers.

I send her the photograph. She replies in seconds.

Ewww. Grim :/ xxx

Two kisses means best friends. Besties. Three means more than that.

I put the photo up on Insta.

She's the first to like it.

I float round the house for the rest of the day. Ants forgotten.

'Put it away, man!'

I look down at my crotch with shock-horror eyes. Wave jazz hands at the lads.

Colm upends his Bombay potatoes with laughing; splotches of turmeric on the white tablecloth. Why do they bother with white tablecloths here? My hand's over my phone, swift as a gunslinger. I look up and Benny's shaking his head at me.

She doesn't text till I get home, until I'm in bed, not sleeping, not quite worrying. Not yet.

Good night gorgeous xxx

In the silence I can hear the ants creaking downstairs, crawling over each other.

I think of her instead and brim with warmth.

I've got to wait in today. Men are coming to replace the carpet on the stairs. It's long past it; faded and saggy like skin. Old roses bloom like fading memories beneath my feet.

I go upstairs, dip my toes into the little cubes of light cast down from the skylight on the way and shut the attic door. It clicks like a metal tut.

I read back through our messages to each other, count kisses all the way down the stairs. I check her Insta; she's liked a photo of a forest; she's shared a video on Facebook, a dog licking a baby penguin's head, Chinese symbols across the top.

It's much later. The house is humming, as if something's happened. The radio won't turn off. One thing after another. There's still ant powder left so I pour it in the corners. Little toxic snowdrifts. Bastards.

My phone buzzes. My lungs clench to fists for a few seconds.

Hey petal :) How you doing today? Xxx

I uncurl my spine on the wooden lips of the stairs and smile. Thumbs out. When I go back upstairs, the attic door is open but the sun is gone. Some of the banisters are broken.

'Will you just leave it?' Benny's knuckles are white. He bares his teeth.

My jalfrezi has formed a thick skin; a red mountain range, peaks and pinnacles of drying meat that point skyward.

I don't feel hungry.

Colm withdraws his fork and glares into the space where his balti was; he won't look at me. In primary when Colm got upset he sat and sulked. Benny shouted.

I go home to get some peace from them, stomach yawning.

I text her before I go to bed.

You ok love? Xxx

I wake up in the night, convinced my phone has gone off; it's still, a little black coffin, 50% full.

The morning staggers home.

She's been on Insta before and after I texted. She's liked a picture of a toddler with paint all over its face; a plate of buttered crumpets from a cafe in York. She's changed her Facebook profile banner; it's got a load of likes, including mine.

She'll text soon.

I begin planning my reply.

I worry about the old carpet, the ants and the attic door.

The attic door is beginning to piss me off.

I do an experiment.

I make a video of the attic door being open, being closed then being open again; I stick it up on Insta with a black and white filter. A ghost emoji.

I'm up at 6am because she's still not texted; nearly threw a mug against the kitchen wall when the kettle wouldn't boil.

She likes a photo of some daffodils in a jam jar and a home-made Easter card by someone's kid. An egg with arms and a zigzag of felt tip pen for a mouth. It looks furious.

I pour bleach into the ants' lair. The ants are nowhere to be seen. It'll kill them in their sleep. I leave my phone on the worktop so it's a surprise when I come back in.

It works.

1 message received.

My heart thunders. All the breath falls out of my mouth.

But it's only Colm. The message he sends every week to me and Benny. I should have known.

Curry night? Be there or be a cock.

I can't think of a reply.

The ants come back as the day dies; little lines of them through the house. Tomorrow I'll buy some grout, block up their holes. I pour more powder over them but they don't give a shit.

No one's liked my video. It only has two views. Both of them are me.

I should go for curry, I think as 7pm becomes 10pm. I should really go.

I remember when we went to the lake, autumn crunching beneath our feet. I remember how I put my arm around her; how she moved up against me, the smell of her. How right it felt, the two of us beneath a low flying sky.

'I really like you.' I said.

Her smile.

Silence haunts these halls.

I change my phone alerts. She's now got her own sound. I close the attic door and jump when I hear it twinkling from my bedroom.

She shares one of those time-lapse food videos on Facebook. *Perfect Bakewell Tart*. She re-tweets a petition to call the government to account.

The attic door is open. The ant powder is still not finished. It's gone from all the corners of the living room. Little bastards.

I do an experiment; no powder, no bleach. I wait till sundown and watch the ants, see where they go.

The kitchen's cold, the window is jammed open an inch. The ants don't care; they head for the spilled sugar on the side. It's soaked up a puddle of tea and formed a crust. The ants are prospectors, grinding away at it. I take a photo and send it to her. Why the fuck not?

I remember our knees touching when we sat beside each other at a theatre. The night we kissed for the first time.

I don't sleep in case she replies.

The carpet people have not been. I watch out the window all day, phone in my hand. A van pulls up and goes away again after a little while. I don't hear the doorbell.

She's liked a picture of a baby with a crumpled, furious face, a video of a bee, its furry arse poking out the lip of a foxglove. Birdsong in the background.

Beans for tea. The hob won't light so I eat them from the tin, cold. The spilled sugar-tea has a trail of ants working at it from midday.

There's no point cleaning it up.

I remember our feet touching beneath the table in a busy bar; hiding smiles with our hands.

I lean a chair against the attic door and come back an hour later. The chair's back downstairs but I can't remember if I did it or not.

There's beans on the kitchen floor. I pour ant powder into them and mix it with a fork. Flies have joined the ants; I wonder what will happen if the flying ants take off and there's a dogfight. I hold my phone up to capture it. Stay still.

By the time night comes, it's not happened.

The ants have finished the sugar and move on to pastures new.

The lads are quiet; Colm chases chicken round his plate with a fork; a trail of balti in its wake. I make a joke about the attic door not closing and Colm's big mouth but neither of them get it.

Benny's on the sick from work, he says.

'Taking it one day at a time, mate.' He says and his eyes are wet.

'Best way for me is just to keep on.' Colm says, looking down at his plate. 'Don't stop to think.'

They stare at my plate.

I ask the waiter where my jalfrezi is but the lads get up to leave. It doesn't matter, I'm not even hungry.

I remember her turning over; her hand on my chest, the smell of her hair. A hole appears in my heart in the shape of her sleeping face.

She's still not texted. I look back through Insta at all the pictures of me that she liked.

I'm scowling at a 'Keep off the grass' sign, sticking out my tongue in my pyjamas. That was only a couple of weeks ago.

I take a few more; some happy, some sad, some neutral; the red light of the Indian in the background. I take one of me pretending to eat Colm's half-finished balti.

When I get home the attic door is open and the ants are at the beans. It's freezing and the heating won't go on, however many times I try. I'll call the repair men tomorrow.

Flies buzz around the bottom of the stairs.

I think I'm being haunted.

There's more flies than ants now. Both parties have migrated to the bottom of the stairs. The carpet men still haven't come. The repair men's number won't connect.

She's not texted.

She likes a photo collage of a couple who I don't know, grinning, kissing over glasses of fizz, *Happy Anniversary*. My heart heaves; that could have been us, I think, that could have been us one day. I write that out in a text, address it to her then delete it.

I check all the cupboards. There's plenty of food. The fridge is starting to smell but there's tins that'll keep. I wonder if I should go to the supermarket. I might bump into her.

I imagine her turning away, head down, hurrying.

Now she's ghosting me, I don't dare to see her.

I remember the way we used to hold hands, tentative as if what we had wasn't quite real.

I remember how she kissed me, her tongue hungry, like she wanted to devour me. She tasted of roll-ups and rain.

I'd give anything to taste her again.

'It was just one night.' I say. 'Just that one time.'

Colm ignores me. His beard's got longer, grey strands through it now. He's getting better at eating; opens his mouth wider, wipes the rice from it with a napkin.

'One time I missed curry night and I'm sorry.'

Benny shakes his head. He's on a pharl; shovelling it in between sips of lager.

'You should get a lassi, mate.' I say, 'Cool your mouth down.'

He ignores me too.

'I used to have a lassie. Till she started ghosting me,' I say, winking. 'You get it?'

Neither of them laughs.

I thought that was a pretty good one. For me.

I haven't ordered but I'm not hungry. I keep thinking about the smell in the fridge, the flies, the attic door. Her.

I want a bit of poppadom but I've not paid.

I don't want Benny to start shouting.

'I should have come.' I say, staring down at the empty plate before me, the knife and fork lying together on their bed of soft green napkin. 'I should have come that time but I didn't and I'm sorry.'

Both of them are crying now; they drink their lager and shove curry into their mouths so they don't have to speak.

I want to start shouting, I wish I had the guts. I want to ask them is this all because I didn't come for curry that time? Because I chose her over you two? Is that why?

I tell them about the attic door to fill the silence; the ants; the beans. The carpet men who didn't come. Her.

When I look up, they've gone. The lights in the Indian are off and the plates are cleared. Bollywood is silent, radio music floats in from the kitchen. I can smell disinfectant. Someone sings along in Urdu, loud and high, as if no one's there.

She likes a photo of yellow overalls flecked with white paint; a stuffed budgie with wire legs leaning in a cage.

She re-tweets a picture of Donald Trump with mouths for eyes.

I go home to darkness. I get in bed but can't get warm.

'I've not felt like this about anyone for so long.'

Her voice is the whistle of a ghost train that traces tear tracks down my cheeks.

There's still ant powder left. I pour it into the bin. Turn away, gasping from the stink. I need to put the bag out. When I go back in the living room it's back, the ant powder in its tub on the mantelpiece.

I laugh.

I make a video of me laughing.

I throw the ant powder against the wall. It makes no sound. The flies are buzzing in a great black blanket in the hall.

I go to check the attic door but this time I stop and look at whatever it is the insects have found on the stairs.

The flies found it first but there's no war. The creatures share spoils.

I look back through the banisters into the living room. The ant powder's back on the mantle.

The attic door will still be open.

Something's broken at the bottom of the stairs; bloated with rot; bones stick out at its knees and elbows. A line of ants lead from its eyes, its mouth.

The flies rise and fall with an elegant synchronicity like a flock of birds. I feel like I shouldn't be looking. I don't even take out my phone.

There's a pile of junk mail at the door.

I go upstairs one last time. See the place beside the attic door where the carpet came free from its mooring, where it snatched at my foot with its rose-pink claws like the fading memory of a monster. A few of the banisters are broken; splintered as if something fell.

A blotch of brown blood on the landing wall.

Sunlight drips through the skylight onto my toes. It feels like nothing.

I remember when we watched the Christmas choir, side by side in the shopping centre, hiding our tears. Hands clasped tight in my jacket pocket.

1% battery left on my phone.

She likes a picture of balloons; white balloons ascending into a summer sky.

My name on each one.

In the Blink of an Eye
Beda Higgins

BEDA HIGGINS has two collections of short stories. *Chameleon* (IRON Press 2011), was longlisted for the Edgehill Prize, *Little Crackers* (Saraband Press 2014) was longlisted for the Edgehill Prize and the Frank O'Connor Prize 2015. Beda is a recipient of two Northern Writers Awards and has been shortlisted for various other awards. When not writing, Beda works as a qualified Psychiatric and General Nurse. She lives with her husband in Newcastle upon Tyne and has three grown-up children.

ONE THIRTY IN the afternoon, the sun slit a white knife through the curtains, stabbing Jo awake. All staff on the Intensive Care Unit had to do their turn of nights. Night duty didn't suit Jo, she never slept, and tossed and turned in a dreamless twilight. She knew she wouldn't get back to sleep and blearily threw the covers back. She picked up the photo on her bedside table. It was two months and seven days since she'd seen Dan. He was on a six month contract in Buenos Aires. She kissed his photo. 'Only one more shift before I see you.' She kissed it again. 'I can't wait.'

The last night on duty was a quiet one, she'd almost fallen asleep in the dull early hours. The ambulance man's urgent message jolted her awake. 'We've picked up a young lad, looks like meningitis. He's in a bad way, we're bringing him straight up to you. You'll have to act fast on this one.'

They ran, wheeling him into ITU. The doctor took one look at the boy's florid rash and yelled, 'IV antibiotics now!'

Jo's hands shook, she tried to carefully draw up the mixture but her needle came off, it wasn't fastened on properly, the antibiotics spilt all over the place.

'Come on hurry, we're going to lose him. He needs intravenous penicillin now!'

She rubbed her face and clumsily drew up the second vial, her fingers were clothes pegs, the antibiotic mixture squirted, dribbling down her shaking hands. She handed the syringe to the doctor, it was half the dose it should've been and not mixed properly.

The doctor shot into the vein, but the boy's eyes were clouding. They waited for a response. 'We're losing him,' he said through gritted teeth. The boy's terrified eyes froze, locked on Jo's, and remained, fixed and dilated.

They did their best to resuscitate him; pummelling and shoving him full of needles, pumping his body with electricity, limbs jerking with every shock, but the heart monitor remained flat. He was seventeen years old, the same age as Jo's kid brother.

The doctor stormed off the unit. If she'd been quicker, more efficient, if she hadn't been half asleep, if she'd got the antibiotics drawn up a few minutes earlier – might it have made a difference? Again and again she asked herself, would those three minutes have saved his life?

She had to lay him out while listening to the parents' racking sobs in the visitors' room. She gently sponged his young supple skin, it seemed so alive, but was so cold. She spoke to him quietly, wishing more than anything that she'd been quicker because maybe...

Last of all she reached to close his eyes, her trembling hand hovered, she couldn't do it; he had beautiful eyes.

The flight to South America was hellish. She was sandwiched between two booze hounds who would share yet another hilarious joke, shaking her awake every time she almost dropped off.

She didn't see Dan until he was bouncing next to her in the arrivals. 'Welcome to Buenos Aires.'

'Christ Dan when did you grow that?' She stood back to take him in properly. 'No wonder I didn't see you coming.'

'Don't you like it?' He stroked his luxurious beard.

'It's, well, it's ridiculous.'

He didn't care and swung her round laughing. 'That's my girl, never mince your words.' He grabbed her hand and took her case in the other. 'Come on we'll get a taxi, what d 'you fancy doing?'

'I'd like to have a long shower and sleep.' She yawned. 'I'm knackered.'

He ruffled her hair. 'Course you are.'

His apartment was small and functional. He held her close. 'Do you have to sleep first?'

She felt sticky and unwashed, the beard tickled close up. 'Yes I do.'

She couldn't sleep, it was hot and humid. She had a headache; day and night merged.

Dan knocked gently and brought her coffee. 'Feeling any better?'

'Not really, but you look better. You didn't have to, but I'm glad. It didn't seem like you.' She touched his smooth cheek.

'I can always grow it again when you go back. What d 'you fancy doing today?'

'You decide, take me round the city or to something I'll like.'

They got the underground. He happily held her hand. 'You'll like it here. The people are friendly and easy going.'

They ran down the subway stairs. It was hot, the air clinging in grimy droplets. The train was packed, skins on skin, sucking apart as passengers moved on. She was immersed in different stages of BO; days, weeks, she tried to breathe through her mouth. Dan led her out of the carriage and up the stairs. The streets bustled, a place of a thousand hands with eyes and mouths moving and pawing, tugging, shoving and jostling.

She felt a rush of heat, the world closing in on her. 'I need some air Dan,' her voice trembling.

He put his arm around her and guided her across the road, while snatching sideways glances. He led her towards a park; less people, more air. 'You okay now?'

She nodded, her racing heart settling.

They sat on a bench and Dan asked softly, 'What kicked that off?'

Jo bit her lip, gazing into the distance, keeping her silence. Dan frowned but didn't push it.

In the middle of the park was a large metal monument in the shape of a flower. 'What d'you think of that?' he asked.

'It reminds me of the Triffids.'

'Fantastic isn't it? It's made from old war planes from the Falkland War. It's a symbol of Argentina. At night the flower actually opens up with light, it's beautiful.'

'You're kidding? It's a big hunk of metal symbolising war, and war equals death. I get enough of that at work.' She turned away from it. 'Take me somewhere fun.'

He smacked his thighs. 'We'll go to the Bodegella area. It's where the port used to be. Now it's a bohemian hotspot, and a great shopping market.'

The market was like a shipwreck above water; shoals of people swam over, under, and around her. So many eyes and noises drumming, voices caterwauling. She grasped his arm. 'I'm sorry, I need to get away Dan, it's too much.'

He guided her to a small park. She rubbed her head. 'I'm sorry, I haven't slept properly for ages. I'm really jumpy.'

She didn't want to tell him about the seventeen-year-old boy haunting her head, but he was there, always. She'd seen him on the subway, at the market, in the park, every young healthy body swinging by taunted her. 'A museum or art gallery might be nice.' She wanted to be distracted, to forget.

'The Belle Artes gallery has a great selection,' said Dan, 'European, South American, traditional and modern.'

Jo stared and stared at the meaningless modern art, willing herself to find something in the splodges. Dan whispered, 'It's trying to force the viewer to consider an alternative way of looking at life.' He held her hand, entwining fingers.

'When did you become a cultural guru?' she asked.

'I want to share with you.'

Jo narrowed her eyes, *I don't know you anymore.*

They went upstairs where there was an exhibition of Goya paintings.

The room was dark. Jo shivered staring at a monkey baring its teeth in a corner of hell. She moved on, the eyes seemed to follow. Each painting was eerily illuminated to enhance glimpses of the underworld. Death danced deliriously on the canvass. A skeletal hand lay across a white breast, squeezing the flesh. The doctor had uselessly squeezed and thumped the boy's mottled skin. She was swept along in a tsunami of panic and hurried to get out of the room, forcing herself not to run.

She slumped on a bench in the corridor and dropped her head in her hands, thankful for bright light and noise.

Dan came out from the exhibition a few minutes later. 'Hey, I've been looking for you. You missed the last lot.'

'My head's too full. I couldn't concentrate anymore.'

'That's the power of real art, like I was trying to explain.'

'Can we get a drink?' She rubbed her temples.

They went to the café. 'The one with the skeleton hand reaching forward, it was so real,' she said, 'it freaked me out.'

'I don't remember the skeleton.' Dan frowned.

'You must, it was so powerful – next to the depiction of hell with the monkey baring its teeth.'

Dan laughed. 'I don't remember a monkey either. Were we at the same exhibition?'

'D'you think I'm seeing things?' she snapped.

'Jo, calm down.' Dan stroked her hand. 'You're a bit uptight Sweetheart. I guess next time I'll have to pay more attention.'

'Sorry,' Jo waved, 'I know I'm snappy. I had a crap time at work before I came out here.'

'D'you want to talk about it?'

She shook her head. 'Not now.'

'Okay, let's lighten the mood. I'm going to take you to the cemetery next.' He kissed her.

'You are kidding me?'

'It's a big tourist attraction, fascinating place. Wealthy Argentinians buy a space to have their coffins placed there. Some of the statues are incredibly ornate, pieces of art in their own right.'

'It sounds morbid, looking at dead plots.'

'It's not, it's a hoot.' He smiled. 'It's like a ride on the ghost train at Blackpool; tacky kitsch.'

He went to the counter to pay for the coffee, and laughed with the bloke. Jo watched him moving his hands in a way she wasn't familiar with. She stared at his tanned, smiling face. Dan had changed, or maybe she had.

At the cemetery Dan looked around for information. 'I'll nip over to the shop and buy a guidebook, you wait here.'

An old, wiry woman stepped towards Jo. Her seemingly child-like body was totally at odds with her wrinkled leathery skin. Long greying hair flowed down her back in coarse waves. Her beetle black eyes shone, surrounded in a concertina of wrinkles. She smiled, 'Welcome, welcome, welcome indeed.' She bowed formally. 'I hope you enjoy our cemetery.' She placed a small bony hand on Jo's arm whispering, 'Head for the back of the cemetery my dear, far more interesting.' She turned and strolled away.

Dan came back with the guide book. 'Eva Peron's plot is over here.' He pointed.

'Let's go towards the back instead,' Jo nodded, 'it's less touristy.'

'Okay,' Dan shrugged.

They weaved through the higgledy-piggledy maze of statues, graves, caskets old and new. Angel figures stood tall and wide-winged over glass caskets, straddling the ground, half in and half out of the earth. Waxy figures lay behind glass, their hands crossed over chests, beatific faces. The sun sluiced through the labyrinth.

Dan jumped up on a statue wrapping his arm around its neck. 'There's a fine line in South America between the living and the dead. This place is a hammed up half-way house.' He took a selfie with the old statue.

Jo stared at the garish caskets poking out from the ground. She muttered, 'They're too near. I could touch the cadavers if I wanted to.' She shivered and wandered on alone while Dan snapped photos. She came to a new freshly chiselled statue. It was exquisitely crafted, she touched the smooth white marble, warmed in the strong sun. The limbs were long and lean, the fingers and toes round crescents of perfection. She followed the taut torso up and felt an ache; the young boy's chest bruised by fists trying to beat life back into him. *If only I'd got the antibiotics to him sooner, he might have had a chance.*

'Check out the date,' Dan studied the statue, 'he's a fresh one. Stay there and I'll get a photo.' He glanced at the phone and back at the statue. 'I don't understand,' he frowned, 'look,' he showed Jo the snap he'd taken, 'it says the statue blinked.'

She looked up, the statue stared at her, his angry eyes wide open.

The Follow Up
Tom Johnstone

TOM JOHNSTONE works as a gardener, and enjoys extreme lawn-mowing (though not as extreme as in the story published herein!). His fiction has appeared in various publications, including *Best Horror of the Year #8* (Night Shade Books), and the anti-austerity anthology he co-edited with the late Joel Lane, *Horror Uncut*, was nominated for the 2015 British Fantasy Award. More information at <tomjohnstone.wordpress.com>.

THE OTHER THREE are hand mowing with the small, pedestrian John Deeres. I ride the big John Deere. They follow me like ducklings after their mother. Same pea-green livery, with a small, yellow leaping deer design. My John Deere ride-on is a massive beast. I sit high above the other three, as befits my higher grading. They hunch over the dead man's handles of their walk-behind John Deeres, doing the follow-up, cutting the patches of grass I can't get into, cutting close to walls and stones, fences and trees, ducking under low-hanging branches that would hit me in the face at the speed I'm travelling and the height I'm sitting. Sometimes they cut these awkward, fiddly bits ahead of me, though it's still called follow-up. Don't ask me why. You might as well ask me why the lock-up where we keep the mowers is called the ghost store. It's just one of those things. It is what it is.

When they do go ahead of me, the other three, they often cut more than they need to, second-guessing what I can and can't do. Sometimes they cut bits that I would have gone ahead and done if I'd got a head start on them.

I prefer the times when I start mowing an hour or so before them. I can knock out a few acres before breakfast. The grass sprays out from the back of my machine like green rain. Of course, dog-walkers don't always pick up after their pets, so then it's more like brown rain. Everyone loves the smell of cut grass in the summer, but not when it's got a whiff of dogshit in it! You don't want to be standing too close behind it then. You don't want to be standing in front of it either, mind you...

When it's been raining a lot, it's a struggle. The grass is long and wet. Also, you get frogs and that lying up in there, and then, well, it's red rain. It's like that joke about the frog in a blender.

The blades of this machine are quite similar to a blender's, come to think of it. It's not a cylinder mower: they have a scissor-type action, with the grass cleanly sliced between the blade and a kind of block or anvil. Not this machine. Not the John Deere 1445 Series II, four-wheel-drive. This machine's got rotary blades, which spin round and just smash the grass up. Its sixty-litre capacity tank means it can run more than ten hours without refuelling. The integrated roll-over protection structure provides maximum safety. This isn't the only safety feature either. There are weights that must be attached to the machine to act as ballast, so the mower doesn't tip over when you raise the deck for cleaning and maintenance of the rotary blades. There is a flashing yellow light to warn members of the public and your colleagues of your approach.

Which makes it all the more surprising, what happened.

Despite the yellow beacon, you still get idiots in the parks who get in your way. Like the ones who carry on sunbathing or sleeping rough or whatever until you get right close to them, daring you to slice and dice them before they'll deign to move to another bit of grass. It's like they expect you to mow around them then come back another day to finish off the body-shaped portion of uncut grass you've left. Imagine if I did that! There'd be hundreds of green body shapes all over the park, like those chalk marks you get in murder thrillers and that.

Of course, sunbathers aren't too much of a problem here. After all, who wants to sunbathe in a graveyard? The main hassle is dog-walkers, especially the ones that let their dogs off the lead when you're mowing, so you have to keep an eye out for their pooches running up to the mower, yapping and getting in the way. I can see one now. Can't see the owner though. It's running around down the far end, near the willow tree. *That* willow tree. It's a border collie, I think. I hope it doesn't come any closer. Its face looks all wrong from here. That's not the only reason though. They get in the way.

Time for a fag break. Maybe by the time I've had a smoke, the dog will have gone. I turn the engine off. I glance over to the van. The other three are loading their walk-behind John Deere mowers back onto the van. (C52KS models with a 52cm cutting length, an external 7 litre fuel tank, AVS and a single-speed drive system.) Two of them are climbing into the van, ready to go to the next job. I break off from rolling my fag, calling to them that the follow-up here isn't finished yet. There's a band of uncut grass around the edge next to the fence-line, tufts of grass gone feathery in the dry weather. No way would I be able to get any closer to the fence without knocking into it, and possibly damaging it, not to mention the John Deere itself!

One of the lads is coming over. I don't look up. I pretend to be concentrating hard on my roll-up, taming the unruly brown fibres with my fingers and the cigarette paper. He's saying someone's already done this bit. Really? I'm saying, without looking up. Who did it then? I didn't see anyone here. And the other three didn't go ahead of me. I had a head-start on them, and they've only just caught me up.

He just stands there, waiting for me to return eye-contact. I only look up when I've finished rolling my fag. I look at him, then at the ground. I see the line, the slight groove left by the wheel of a walk-behind mower. A John Deere C52KS? Or is it a Victa? Lighter and easier to manoeuvre, but less reliable, less durable. The firm's rickety old Victas have been condemned. The grease monkeys can't get parts for them any more when they break down. Last time we had a Victa on our gang was before –

Did I say that aloud? He's still standing there, looking down at the line of grass. There are some feathery bits sticking up, but just a few, I now see. They could be the scraps that inevitably get missed even when hand-mowing tight-close to a fence like this one.

But there is a line from a lawn mower wheel.

Still, I'm not going to admit that to him. I tell him to go over it just in case. As he's finishing it, with the other two watching, bemused, I use this opportunity to get ahead of them and start on the cemetery. There'll be a lot of follow-up needed here, what with all the tombstones and trees and what not. One of the lads'll need to use a strimmer to get really close. Still, there's enough space between the obstacles for me to get around on the John Deere.

This is where it happened of course.

But I don't let that bother me. You have to move on. I'm just going to crack on with it, just the same as I do every fortnight at this time of year. It's like I'm one with the machine. I know this mowing round like the back of my hand. London cab drivers call their training The Knowledge. Well, that's what this is like. Sometimes, I see butterflies come flying out from where I've cut the grass. I don't like it when that happens. I know some of them must get shredded by the whirling blades. The ones that get out might be crippled by tiny scratches on their fragile wings. But I can't stop for every butterfly, can I? Sounds stupid, but I often think that little leaping yellow deer on the John Deere trademark looks as if it's leaping for its life to get away from a John Deere mower!

Stupid.

There's that dog again! Just when I thought it had gone. Definitely a border collie, looking at the coat. Not the face though. The face is nothing like a border collie's. Come to think of it, it doesn't look like any dog's face I've ever seen.

I need to concentrate. I know what can happen when you lose concentration. I try to clear my mind of all distractions. There's just me, my machine and the whispery grass.

There is one thing that's distracting me though. It seems as if someone's already done the follow-up. I can see bands of cut grass next to the fences, around trees and tombstones. Who's done that then? The other three can't be here yet.

It is what it is.

I'm going to crack on with it, scattering grass, dandelion leaves and small insects in my wake. I'm not even going to look at that over-hanging willow tree next to the now filled-in hole where it happened, even though I caught a glimpse of long, black hair in its dappled shade. It was in the corner of my eye though. It was gone when I looked straight at it.

What's done is done.

I'm racing through it now. It helps that it hasn't rained for a couple of weeks, so the grass is thin and light, but even if it was wet, I'd still get through it, no trouble. The hydraulic deck drive means a constant speed even in tough conditions. Along with the low-rated engine speed and advanced exhaust system, they also make this machine noticeably quiet.

Not so quiet that no one can hear you coming.

Unless they're wearing ear defenders. Like she was that day. I told her not to, said she needed to be aware of everything going on around her. She said she wanted to protect her hearing from tinnitus and that. She always wanted everything her way. Didn't want to strim around the tombstones, had to mow. Only liked mowing with a Victa. The John Deere pedestrian mowers are heavy, mind you. One man can just about lift a Victa by himself, but not a John Deere C52KS. That day, I persuaded her to try the John Deere pedestrian mower, saying it was less noisy. That way she wouldn't need to wear ear defenders.

'Anyway', I said, 'you'll ruin your lovely hair, wearing them.'

I said it with a twinkle in my eye, I thought. Still gave me a dirty look though. I was only paying her a compliment!

I suppose she didn't like compliments, not coming from me anyway, though I meant it about her lovely, long, black hair.

That decided her. She was going to wear the ear defenders.

She was like that. Bit obstinate. Wouldn't be told. She was a grafter though. I'll give her that! I think she had something to prove, something to do with being a woman in this job, where it's mainly blokes. So she'd push herself, that little bit too hard now I come to think of it. Don't be such a dog's body, I used to say.

Speaking of which, there's that border collie again.

Come to think of it, she said something about owning a border collie. I remember when it happened, I was discussing with the lads what would happen to the animal.

If only she'd listened. Some things are worse than tinnitus. And for all her talk of health and safety, she didn't wear a high-viz jacket.

The dog's getting closer. That face. I don't like the look of that.

I need to crack on. I want to get this finished before nine.

The hydraulic drive whatnot might be fairly quiet, but it's loud enough that I can barely hear what the vicar's saying as he waves me to stop. I turn off the engine to see what he wants: first I push the PTO switch to the off position; then I move the throttle lever to the slow idle position; I lock the park brake, lower the mowing deck to the ground, a pea-green, wedge-shaped attachment on two wheels, a bit like the head of a hammerhead shark; finally, I turn the ignition key to the stop position and remove it. I can see the vicar's gesturing for me to get down from the buttercup yellow seat. The machine is on a slope, but I could get down. The park brake enables the operator to do this, though it is advisable to test it by stopping the machine on a seventeen degree slope: if it moves more than 61 cm in an hour, the brakes need adjusting. I'd say this was a steeper gradient than that. Anyway I'm not going to get down.

The vicar is a youngish man with red hair. I look at him enquiringly. He asks me to pass on his thanks to the young lady who cut the grass in his little bit of garden behind the vestry. I listen to his high, piping voice, with a hint of Geordie, saying she had long, black hair, and a little border collie with her. I want to punch him. Is he taking the mick? He must be new to the parish. Doesn't he know there's no young lady on our mowing gang? Not any more.

I tell him this. There's a moment of confusion. There's a pounding behind my temples, a throbbing. He says maybe she was from another department. I say maybe she was.

I look at the willow with its overhanging branches, the ones that blinded me that day, so I didn't see her. Maybe I might have done if she'd been wearing a high-viz. Maybe she might have heard me in time to get out of my way if she hadn't been wearing ear defenders. Maybe if the council had paid the money for proper surveyors, rather than sending one of the lads down with a rusty metal rod to check for subsidence, the ground wouldn't have opened up and swallowed her into the old workhouse grave. Maybe if she'd been using a Victa instead of a John Deere C52KS, I'd have been able to lift up the mower that was pinning her down there and she might have got away with a broken rib.

Maybe.

There was no one else around, either to help me lift the mower off her, or to see that it was the knock from the ride-on that pushed her, mower and all, onto the dodgy ground. The dead man's handle meant the blades didn't carry on spinning when the mower fell in after her, so she might still be alive when we got it off her. Even without the mower on top of her, I would have needed help to dig out all the soil that had fallen onto her. When I finally managed to get help, I said that was how I found her. I've never told anyone any different, not during the hearing. I thought I was going to lose my ride-on mower ticket, my meal ticket. No more being at one with my machine. There were no other witnesses. Apart from her. And she wasn't at the hearing of course, thought I kept glimpsing long, black hair in the corner of my eye as the coroner questioned me.

But it is what it is. What's done is done. There was nothing more I could have done.

I disengage the park brake, and drive the ride-on to where the others are cutting an area that's barred to me by an iron fence, its gateway too narrow for me to enter. I can see them in the distance. Something's not quite right. I turn the John Deere round, start heading back to the yard, a roll-up in my mouth. I'm done here. Usually, I'd have my smoke while the mower was stationary, when I've finished. Not this time. I just want to get back. Whenever I glance round to check the traffic behind me, I glimpse a dog trotting along on the pavement behind me. A border collie with a human face, a thread of saliva dangling from its panting jaws as it struggles to keep pace with me.

A woman's face.

I speed up until eventually I outrun the dog. Finally, I'm back at the yard. I open the ghost store to put away the John Deere. But why is there a Victa in there? And why did I keep counting four people mowing the whispering grass behind the gate?

The Last Bus Home
Andrea Stephenson

ANDREA STEPHENSON is a writer and libraries manager from North Shields, where she lives with her partner of 21 years and a Border Terrier. Her stories have been published in *Popshot* and *Firewords* magazines and in the *Aesthetica Creative Writing Annual*. Andrea is inspired by nature, the coastline and the turn of the seasons and writes about creativity, magic and nature at <www.harvestinghecate.wordpress.com>.

SHE WAS ALONE at the bus stop on Roseberry Road. It was the last bus of the night and I was tired and ready to go home. I had no other passengers and had hoped for a clear run. I remember thinking she wasn't dressed for the weather. The pink mini-dress barely covered her limbs and the wind caused her hair to whip around her in dark ribbons. When she got on the bus, I could see the goose pimples on her arms.

'Please take me to Briarwood,' she said, voice shaking with the cold.

'£2.60,' I said, ringing it up.

'No. Please, I've got no money. I had my purse stolen but please, I've got to get home.' I studied her. She had no bag or jacket in which to conceal anything. It might be a scam, but this was a lonely stop and she seemed sort of desperate.

'Alright. Just this once,' I said, beckoning her on.

'Thank you,' she said, and the relief in her face made me think she was genuine.

I glanced back at her a few times in the mirror as we made our way through the night. Nobody else got on and the last time I looked at her, she was slumped into the seat, head resting against the window, as though asleep.

Briarwood was a few stops from the end of the line. I stopped there automatically, remembering the destination, but when I looked in the mirror I couldn't see her. I turned in my seat to look along the bus. Nobody there. That was strange. We hadn't stopped anywhere – nobody else had got on and there was no-one else on the bus to get off. I got out of my seat and made my way up the bus, beginning to panic in case I found her unconscious on the floor or something. There was no trace of her.

I walked up and down the bus twice. I checked the emergency exit. It was closed and when I opened it, just to check, the alarm sounded as it should – she couldn't have got out that way without me knowing about it. Eventually, there was nothing left to do but carry on to the last stop and then the depot. Just before I got off, I checked again, in case there was some place she could be hiding, though I knew it was fruitless. She'd just disappeared. Or maybe I'd imagined the whole thing.

I thought about her regularly over the next week or so. I considered telling one of the other drivers about it, but being new and a woman, I didn't want to give them any ammunition for teasing or anything else. So, I kept it to myself and eventually, I forgot about it.

The next time I did the Briarwood route I couldn't help but remember her. It was one of those nights when things didn't seem to flow. There were some awkward passengers and I couldn't seem to concentrate on what I was doing. A few times I handed over the wrong change and more than once I couldn't remember the right codes for the stops. It wasn't until the end of the night, when I was beginning the last run that I realised that the churning in my stomach had gotten worse. I drove the route in a daze, my guts feeling heavier the closer I got to Roseberry Road. A few stops before I got there, a couple got on. I thought that might make it better, but it actually made it worse. By the time I got to Roseberry Road, I was shaking.

I drove slowly along the road, sure that I'd see her at the bus stop when I reached it. I even stopped. But she wasn't there. I got out of my seat and made a pretence of checking the display on the front of the bus while I looked around me. Nobody. I should have felt better. What had happened last time was odd. I couldn't explain how she'd disappeared, but why that would make me think she'd be there again tonight, I didn't know. Whenever I'm nervous, I feel it in my stomach and that night, it churned all of the way home.

The third time I did that route, I had myself under control. It was as though her not being there the last time had put my worries to rest, so I wasn't paying as much attention. There'd been a bit of activity on the bus, but by the time I got to Roseberry Road, it was empty again. I really didn't think she'd be there, but as I approached, I saw movement in the vicinity of the bus stop. Sure enough, there she was. She wore the same dress. Her hair blew about her in ribbons as it had the last time. I considered driving straight past. I don't know why. What could be so scary about a young girl alone at a bus stop? Still, it was only in the last moments that I slowed down and I sighed deeply before opening the doors.

I noticed the goose bumps on her arms again as she came towards me.

'Please take me to Briarwood,' she said.

Exactly the same words. Exactly the same desperate expression.

'£2.60,' I said, but I didn't ring it through this time.

'No. Please, I've got no money. I had my purse stolen but please, I've got to get home.'

'Is this some kind of scam?' I said.

She just looked at me.

'A few weeks ago. Same time, same place. You told me exactly the same story. I let you on and you disappeared.'

She blinked slowly.

'Please take me to Briarwood,' she said.

'What's going on?' I said. 'Tell me who you are and what you're playing at.'

She blinked again. 'Please take me to Briarwood,' she repeated.

'And what if I say no?' I asked.

She said nothing, only stood there, silently blinking. I didn't know what to do. We stayed as we were, me sitting in my seat staring at her, she just looking at me blinking, as the wind blew in and chilled us both. But there was something in the pit of my stomach that stopped me from throwing her off the bus.

'Ok,' I said and beckoned her on. 'But sit at the front.'

She did as she was told and I took as many looks as I could at her as we rode on. Eventually, she adopted the same sleeping posture as before, but still, I watched her as often as I could while driving. I was convinced that this time she wouldn't disappear on me. Just before we got to Briarwood, I checked and she was still there. I pulled up at the stop, looked in the mirror and she was gone. I cursed myself. I'd only taken my eyes off her for a moment, but it was a moment too long. I sat at the stop for a while, then, without enthusiasm, I checked the bus again to see if she was hiding. But I knew it was hopeless before I even started. She had vanished again.

I tried to avoid that route after that. I didn't put into words why, either with my bosses or with myself. I just did all I could to swap routes, or swap shifts, so that I didn't have to make that lonely journey and risk seeing her again. Again, I thought about asking the other drivers if they'd come across her, but I couldn't open myself up to the humiliation. But eventually, I knew it would come round again and it did. As luck would have it, it was snowing that night.

That meant there weren't many passengers, but it did mean that one of the other drivers hitched a ride back to the depot with me. I was pleased because that meant she wouldn't show her face. Still, I couldn't help feeling unsettled as we started along Roseberry Road. I carried on half-heartedly chatting with Alan, the other driver, but I could already feel the tension in my stomach. And did I just imagine it, or had he gone a bit quiet too?

Our conversation ceased as we got close and to my surprise, I caught a glimpse of the pink dress. I didn't know what to do. Should I stop or should I not? If I didn't he might report me for not picking up a passenger, but if I did, what would happen then? I began to slow, but at the last moment, I put my foot down and moved past the bus stop.

'What are you doing?' Alan said quickly. 'There's a passenger, you have to stop.'

I shook my head. 'Not for her,' I said.

'You have to stop,' Alan said, his voice rising.

'It's a scam,' I said. 'I've stopped for her before. Twice. She says she's got no money, but it's just a scam.'

'Stop the bus,' he said.

'What?'

'I said stop the bus. You have to go back.'

'I can't go back now,' I said, 'it's too late. She can get the next one.'

He shook his head and grabbed my arm. 'She can't. It's the last bus. You know that. You've got to go back.'

The look on his face unsettled me. I pulled in to the side of the road.

'What's going on?' I said.

'Just go back. Pick her up. Please,' he said. He kept looking behind us, searching for her in the darkness. 'Quickly,' he said.

I shook my head, but something in the way he said it made me waver. Sighing, I turned the bus around at the next roundabout and went back. As we passed, I could see she wasn't at the stop. I turned around again, back onto the route and pulled up. She wasn't there.

Alan got off the bus. 'Michelle,' I heard him shout into the darkness. 'Your bus is here. Michelle!'

She didn't appear. He got back on, head down and as I made to start driving again he stopped me.

'You can't,' he said.

'What are you talking about?'

'You can't drive now. You didn't pick her up.'

I sighed. 'Are you going to tell me what this is all about?'

'Don't you recognise her?' he said. I shook my head.

'Well, I suppose you're too young,' he said. I waited, gripping the steering wheel.

'That's Michelle Douglas. Does the name mean anything?' I shook my head again.

'It was ten years ago,' he said. 'She was waiting for the last bus home, been out for a night in Erengate. Only she never got home. Afterwards, when they were trying to piece it together, one of the lads remembered her waiting there for the bus. She asked to go to Briarwood. Said she'd lost her purse and didn't have any money. He refused to take her. Thought she was trying it on. He was the last person to see her.'

'What happened?'

'Nobody knows. She was never found. Still missing. After all this time, probably presumed dead. And – well, you saw her didn't you? She must be, otherwise why would she keep appearing, trying to catch the last bus home?'

'So she's a *ghost*?' I said it dismissively, but I could feel the churning in my stomach again.

'You tell me,' he said. 'All I know is she appears, gets on the bus, but she's never there to get off at the other end. Everyone knows about it.'

'Except me.' I said.

'Well, someone should have warned you,' he shrugged.

'What about the driver?'

'Doesn't matter,' he said.

'I think it does, what happened to the driver? Was he involved in it?'

Alan shook his head violently. 'No. No. It wasn't him, whatever happened. But if he'd let her on, you see...'

'It wouldn't have happened.'

'She'd have got home. Safe and sound.' He was quiet for a moment. I looked into the darkness and the wind made me shiver. I slammed the button to close the doors. The hiss of them closing brought Alan back to me.

'He came back to work eventually. The driver. Tom Henderson, he was called. Was never the same. They wouldn't let him drive this route. But one night, he swapped with some newbie who didn't know the score. They found him, crashed at the end of Roseberry Road.'

'What happened?'

Alan shrugged. 'All they know is that he swerved. There was no CCTV then, but you could tell by the tyre tracks. He swerved to avoid something.'

'And what do *you* think happened?'

'How can I know?' he said, irritably.

'So why were you so desperate to pick her up?'

'We just do,' he said. 'Everyone picks her up.'

'You think she caused the accident?'

'As I say, everyone picks her up.'

Hearing him say it irritated me. Made me flippant. So she was a ghost. It was a sad story. But why the superstition? Next time I'd know and I'd decide for myself whether or not to pick her up. He tried to stop me, but I started driving. What was I supposed to do, just sit at the bus stop all night?

I only caught a glimpse of dark hair and pink fabric, darting across the road in front of me. I heard Alan shout something, but it was too late. Instinct made me swerve to avoid her. Everything slowed down to the point that I knew, as the bus started sliding, that it was her, looking for revenge because I'd left her to die in the snow.

But I was fine. I was strapped in to the seat. Whiplash, but nothing more. Alan wasn't strapped in. He was standing next to me, talking. Severe head injuries. He was alive when the ambulance came, but dead by the time he got to the hospital. I didn't drive that route again. Didn't drive any route again. I couldn't get the image of Alan's broken body out of my head. The only thing I'll ever drive now is my little car. And at all costs, I avoid Roseberry Road.

IRON Press is among the country's longest
established independent literary publishers.
The press began operations in 1973 with IRON
Magazine which ran for 83 editions until 1997.

Since 1975 we have brought out a regular list
of poetry, fiction and drama including various
anthologies ranging from *The Poetry of Perestroika*,
through *Limerick Nation*, *100 Island Poems* and the
IRON Book of New Humorous Verse.

We are also one of the leading independent
publishers of haiku in the UK.
Since 2013 we have run a regular IRON Press
Festival round the harbour in our native Cullercoats.

We are delighted to be a part of
Inpress Ltd, which was set up by Arts Council
England to support independent literary publishers.
Go to our website (www.ironpress.co.uk)
for full details of our titles and activities.